Finding the PATH

Finding *the* # PATH

A Novel for Parents of Teenagers

Jeffrey P. Kaplan, Ph.D. & Abby Lederman, M.Ed.

 Hawk
Mountain
Press

Norristown, PA

Front cover photo by Kip Brundage

To order additional copies of this book, contact:
Hawk Mountain Press
P.O. Box 1721
Norristown, PA 19404-1721

Or on the Internet at: www.manageteens.com

E-mail the authors at: *Findingthepath@manageteens.com*

Publisher's Cataloging-in-Publication Data
Kaplan, Jeffrey P.
    Finding the path : a novel for parents of teenagers / Jeffrey P. Kaplan and
    Abby Lederman. — Norristown, PA : Hawk Mountain Press, 2002, c2001.

        p. ; cm.
    ISBN 0-9720358-0-X

    1. Parenting—Fiction. 2. Teenagers—Fiction. 3. Adolescent psychology—
    Fiction. I. Lederman, Abby. II. Title.

PS3611.A753 F56   2002   2002108756
813.6   —dc21   0209

PROJECT COORDINATION BY BOOKPUBLISHING.COM

Printed in the United States of America

06 05 04 03 02 • 5 4 3 2 1

Dedication

To Annie, Max, Tim, Scott and Free, who taught me the power of unconditional love. AML

To all parents and their children who seek to forget fear and remember love, and to my parents, who taught me both. JPK

Contents

Fall

Spring

Introduction

By Abby Lederman

Being drawn into crisis by the anti-social, destructive behaviors of a teenage child is the greatest fear of most parents of pre-adolescent children today. It is also the challenge that motivates Jeffrey P. Kaplan, Ph.D., to get out of bed every morning. After a night that may include calls from distraught teens as late as one or two in the morning, rising to the challenge of yet another day can't be a cakewalk for Jeff, yet my impression is that he wouldn't have it any other way. The more difficult the kid, the more he seems to enjoy the challenge.

I first met Jeff several years ago when he was leading initiation weekends for adolescent boys in the Philadelphia area. Our youngest son, Max, had just completed a weekend, and our whole family came to the graduation ceremony to honor his accomplishment. During the ceremony, it quickly became obvious to me that Jeff had a special knack for working with difficult teenage boys, but I wondered if he related as well to adolescent girls. At the time, our sons—although in many ways typical teenagers—weren't hell-raisers like Annie, our 14-year-old daughter, whose oppositional/defiant behaviors were causing major upheavals in our family.

Luckily for all of us, Jeff did see teenage girls in his practice, and Annie took to him right away. Not only was he a good therapist for our daughter, but Jeff became a catalyst for change in our family. He acted as a one-man family empowerment tool. Gaining Annie's trust by taking her to play pool, bowl, or rock climb, he really listened to her problems without making typical adult judgments about her behaviors. He offered advice only when she asked for it. What he did was model *appropriate* adult-teen communication using trust and respect as a foundation for a relationship.

While he worked with our daughter, Jeff taught the adult Ledermans to treat Annie and her brothers in a trusting, adult manner that made us a more loving family. To further our understanding of his approach to childrearing, my husband and I took Jeff's one-day stress management seminar, and I attended his eight-week parenting course. Separately and together, we spent hours with Jeff learning to modify our sometimes over-the-top behaviors so we could interact with our children without losing our tempers and making matters worse.

I credit Jeff with teaching me to be an adult in the true sense of the word. Once I learned to respect Annie as a growing, maturing individual and started giving her my unconditional love and trust, our relationship changed drastically. We turned from adversaries into allies, and our relationship has continued to blossom. She is a delightful young woman now, who graduated a year early from high school to do internships and service work in different parts of the world before heading off to college. I am profoundly thankful to Annie for challenging me to grow along with her and proud of her for choosing a responsible yet unique path.

Several years ago, during a conversation with Jeff, I mentioned my strong desire to help him spread his message of tolerance, love, and letting go to as many parents of teenagers as possible. When it became apparent that we both felt a strong commitment to writing a book based on his therapeutic approach, we started meeting weekly and mapping out the complicated world of teen/parent relationships. After several false starts, it occurred to us that we could better clarify the many nuances and aspects of parenting teenagers in the Twenty-first Century by creating a fictionalized story to illustrate Jeff's philosophy rather than a textbook to explain his theories. Thus *Finding the Path: A Novel for Parents of Teenagers* was born.

Although Nick Farmer and his mother, Anna, are figments of our imaginations, they act in ways that are common to parents and children struggling with growth and separation issues during the difficult years of adolescence. I used my experiences with my three teenagers and Jeff relied on his many years of work with young people to breathe life into the main characters and to make their daily experiences believable.

If you get nothing more from *Finding the Path* than a good story well-told, the novelist in me will be happy, but neither Jeff nor I will be truly satisfied until we change lives, one family at a time. For that reason, we have written endnotes that explain the theory behind the story.

We urge readers to peruse *Finding the Path* their own way. Some may want to read straight through, ignoring the references to endnotes that pepper the text. Others may prefer to stop at the end of a chapter and refer to the endnotes for that section. Still others may wish to read the text through twice, once to enjoy the story, and then again to learn more about the theory behind it.

It is our sincere hope that this book, the workbook, and affirmation cards to follow, and programs on the www.manageteens.com website will greatly benefit parents, their children, and future generations.

Introduction

By Jeffrey Kaplan, Ph.D.

This book was written with deep passion, respect, and gratitude. It was written for parents who are struggling with their teenagers and for parents who want to prevent such struggles. It was written for therapists to use as a tool in working with families, and for educators who often feel overwhelmed by the amount of responsibility they have in teaching today's children. And finally, it was written for the children and for our children's children who will benefit from the humanistic approaches this book teaches.

The approach to parenting presented in this novel is based on what I call a "love (or faith)-based parenting" model, valuing mutual respect between parent and teen, seizing difficult situations as opportunities for growth, and focusing on the positive rather than fearing the negative. *Finding the Path* is not just a technique book about how to deal with certain teenage issues; rather, the book challenges everyone reading it to look deeply at and better him or herself.

Raising teenagers in today's world is trying for everyone. Well-meaning parents who may have had strong positive relationships with their young children are suddenly confronted with a teenager who questions their authority, disobeys household rules, pushes their buttons almost constantly, and verbally challenges them. Parents find that they lack sufficient tools to help them through these difficult times. Loving parents who want to maintain a healthy relationship with their teens must reassess their personal values, question their own authority, and even reexamine unresolved childhood issues with new intensity. I invite you to accept this challenge, not as a threat to your role as a parent but as a gift and invitation to better yourself emotionally and spiritually.

Finding the Path tells the story of Anna Farmer, a mother who learns ways to handle her teenager better with the assistance of a psychologist. However, her deepest learning comes from another child, a sort of spiritual enigma, who challenges her to look in the mirror and see herself as she truly is. Hawk, the wise teenager Anna meets in the park, points out to her that many of her son's negative traits are reflections of her own dislikes about herself. He challenges Anna to take responsibility for herself in a way she has never done before. Out of her love for her son, Anna accepts the challenge, learning about herself and changing her own behaviors despite the personal pain involved. Her son, Nick, responds positively to the "new" Anna, and they both end up living much more peaceful and joy-filled lives. Although effective parenting does not come with guarantees, those who accept the challenge of love-based parenting will undoubtedly learn about themselves and grow emotionally in the process.

Although this book will not solve all your parenting dilemmas, I hope that you find it a source of support and knowledge as you embrace your important role in the life of a teenager. Thank you for taking this step to better yourself and create a more loving environment for your teenage child or those children with whom you work.

Before closing, I wish to express deep gratitude and appreciation to Abby Lederman. This book would have never been written if it were not for Abby's sincere faith in my abilities, persistence in bringing these ideas to paper, strong writing background, and, most importantly, her deep commitment to her family.

Prologue

Nick Farmer swiped at a bead of sweat trickling down the side of his face. His legs itched inside his best trousers and his shirt clung to his chest, but he didn't care about his physical discomfort. Not today. Not here in the garden of the historic Woolrich House, where his mother had spent many happy hours cultivating the plants that now bloomed in the magnificent summer garden. Not when he was sitting with his wife and son, surrounded by a sea of familiar faces from his boyhood, yet feeling totally alone. Not when they had gathered to mourn the loss of Annamarie Farmer. His mother.

Nick wrapped his arms more tightly around his four-year-old son, Jeremy, who dozed peacefully in his lap, and turned to survey the crowd. He spied his mother's best friend, Carol, wiping her eyes with her husband's handkerchief, too upset to meet his gaze. He exchanged glances with Dr. Elliot, the psychologist who had played such an important role during Nick's difficult adolescent years. He waved at Ms. Blackmun, his high school counselor, and acknowledged his mother's editor at Hawk Mountain Press with a nod.

A few moments later, Charles Southeby, chairman of the Historic Trust and his mother's boss, arose and made his way to the podium to begin the ecumenical service.

The silver-haired gentleman spoke in a clipped, patrician voice. "All of us gathered here today were touched in one way or another by Anna Farmer. I had the privilege of working with her for the last fifteen years of her too-brief life. No one who knew this glorious, spiritual woman will ever forget her. She spread her God-given light to all. She was a beautiful person and will be sorely missed." After reading a passage from the Bible, he returned to his seat.

As speaker after speaker paid homage to Anna Farmer's many good deeds, Nick felt himself grow increasingly agitated. He looked out over the manicured lawn to his mother's gardens, the mingled aromas of the blooms and newly turned soil speaking more to him about her true essence than any words could convey. His mother had been a complex person—sometimes needy and abrupt, sometimes understanding and wise—and in her later years she had certainly loved him and his small family unconditionally, but she hadn't been the saint her friends were describing. Nor would she want to be remembered that way.

A loud wail interrupted Nick's thoughts. With a start, Jeremy sat up, arms flailing in front of him.

"A bee stinged me, Daddy," he screeched. Sobbing, he turned to bury his face in the crook of his father's neck.

Nick whispered quieting words into his son's ear, gently rocking the little boy, trying to console him. Feeling his son's stiff back start to relax, Nick knew it would be only a matter of minutes before the little boy's sobs diminished and then vanished. However, before that could happen, he felt a hand clamp down on his shoulder. He twisted in his seat, his gaze fixing on the disapproving eyes of an elderly woman. Leaning forward, she hissed in his ear, "If you can't keep your child quiet, please remove him. I can't hear the service."

The old resentment of authority that had been a mainstay of his adolescent years welled up inside Nick. He fingered the medallion he wore around his neck, feeling the familiar, grooved edges of the dragon design carved into the stone. Taking deep breaths, he counted to three and forced himself to relax. Once he was centered and in control again, he smiled at the cranky old woman. Patting Jeremy's back, he said, "You're right. I'll walk him around until he calms down."

Although Nick found a pleasant stroll in the garden preferable to sitting at the memorial service, his sense of duty made him return to the makeshift chapel on the lawn as soon as Jeremy was back to his usual cheerful self.

Once again seated in the front row of folding chairs with his son tucked in his lap, Nick listened to another glowing tribute to his saintly mother. Anxiety snaked through his insides, and the palms of his hands grew moist. He had to speak and set the record straight before the service ended, but he didn't know how to express the complicated emotions his mother's memory evoked.

As he debated with himself, Nick noticed a lean, angular man of roughly his own age emerge from the back of the crowd to take the podium. Unlike the other mourners, this man was a total stranger to Nick. Although he was dressed casually for a funeral, wearing black jeans, a black T-shirt, and well-worn boots, the man didn't seem out of place. In fact, with his long, flowing black hair and his welcoming expression, he had a presence about him that demanded nothing yet drew everyone's attention.

For a moment, the stranger's empathetic eyes swept over the mourners, his silent acknowledgement of the pain they all shared more powerful than any of the words yet spoken. Once the silence was complete, his quiet, firm voice filled the void.

"Like the rest of you who have spoken so movingly today, I too remember the Anna Farmer who was spiritual and giving, who felt passionately and wrote eloquently about raising teenagers in a troubled world, who gave unselfishly of herself to others in need. But to me Anna was much more than a doer of good deeds. She was someone who struggled mightily with her own close-minded, judgmental attitudes and her resentment over the curves life threw her. I knew the Anna who, rather than honoring her son Nick's struggle to achieve manhood, became fearful and over-protective; who, consumed with guilt because she felt she was a bad mother, often said hurtful things to the person she loved most in the world."

The man's dark, deeply compassionate eyes darted from one face to another, finally coming to rest on Nick's. As the stranger smiled at him, Nick automatically reached for his amulet. A surge of excitement passed through him. Could this unassuming man with the soft voice and kind eyes be Hawk, the spiritual guide his mother claimed had turned her life around so long ago? After disappearing for fifteen years, had the mysterious Hawk returned to say his final farewell to Anna Farmer?

The man's voice dropped to a whisper, yet Nick heard his words as if they were spoken directly into his ear. Holding Nick's gaze, the man continued. "I keep hearing, 'Anna was such a good person,' and I want to ask, 'What defines a good person?' If she had died before performing all her good deeds, would she have been a 'bad' person? The Anna I remember made mistakes, like we all do, but she learned from them and grew from them. Why, during this time of mourning, are we so afraid to celebrate all of who she was?"

Apparently satisfied that he had said what he needed to, the stranger nodded to Nick and winked at Jeremy. He turned and made his way down the garden path to the wrought iron gate, which clanged shut behind him.

Something inside Nick's chest released. A force beyond his control took possession of his body. He handed Jeremy to his wife and went to face his mother's friends and associates and to unburden his heart. He spoke in a voice that was his own, but different.

"What I most admired about my mother was not the good work she did, or her perseverance in getting her book published, or her bravery at facing her own death. What I most admired about her was her willingness to acknowledge her own frailties and to work on herself, treating each new experience—be it good or bad—as a growth opportunity.

"Because Anna Farmer was my mother, my son has a father who will also learn from his mistakes—and move on. I hope that, through me, Jeremy will pass his grandmother's wisdom on to his children. And thus into the future will stretch an unbroken chain of parents who revel in the challenge and opportunity that raising children brings to those willing to accept it."

Nick took a deep breath and returned to his seat. Jeremy immediately climbed back into his lap and began fingering the amulet that hung from his neck.

"Where did you get this, Daddy?"

A warmth diffused Nick's body. Without thinking, he removed the necklace and placed it on Jeremy. Leaning over, he whispered, "Nana got it from the man with the long hair, the man who winked at you. Then she gave it to me. Now I think you should have it."

Jeremy settled back into his father's embrace, weighing the medallion in his cupped hands. "Who was that man, Daddy?"

Nick looked down at his son, smiling as he remembered the day his mother told him about the mysterious youth who had come into her life for a brief period and then disappeared. "He's an old friend of Nana's. His name is Hawk."

Fall

1

The telephone on Anna Farmer's desk rang. And rang. She ignored it, focusing on the spreadsheet she had to update for an eleven o'clock meeting. Gerry, her impatient, often irate boss, had already been in her office once to ream her out for her tardiness, and she certainly wasn't looking for a replay of *that* Maalox moment.

The stubborn caller refused to hang up. After what seemed like the zillionth ring, when Anna couldn't stand the jangling any longer, she picked up. Cradling the receiver between her chin and shoulder, her eyes still riveted on her computer screen, she snapped, "Sullivan Agency."

"Mrs. Farmer?" an all-too-familiar voice asked.

Anna's vision blurred. Her fingers slipped off the keyboard. The neat rows of numbers on the screen no longer seduced her with their orderliness. There was no such thing as order. Order was an illusion— at least in her life. And now things were about to get worse. The question was how much worse. Her son's guidance counselor was on the line, which meant that Nick was in trouble again.

"Mrs. Farmer? Are you there? This is Sylvia Blackmun."

Anna signed wearily. "Yes, Ms. Blackmun. I know it's you. What did my wonderful son do this time?"

9

"I'm so sorry to disturb you at work, but I'm afraid Nick has been suspended for a week. You'll have to come over to the high school and get him."

This was not what Anna needed. Something had to be wrong with that boy. School had been in session less than a month and he was already in trouble. Why couldn't he leave her in peace?

Turning her pent-up rage at her boss and her son—and even at her husband for dying and leaving her with more than she could handle—on the hapless counselor, she spat out, "I don't think so. Tell Nick to walk his sorry butt home, or have one of his juvenile delinquent friends give him a ride. I have a job to do." She slammed down the telephone.

Wishing she were one of those cartoon characters who could decompress by blowing out steam from her ears, Anna stalked over to the coffee machine. With unsteady hands, she picked up the carafe and began pouring herself a cup.

The phone jangled. She jumped, spilling coffee on the new carpet. Gerry would kill her if she put a permanent stain in it. Cursing under her breath, she grabbed a handful of napkins and dropped to her hands and knees to sponge up the mess. Every time the ringer sounded, her anger spiraled upward. By the time she returned to her desk and picked up the receiver, she couldn't have said a civil word to the caller, even if it had turned out to be the Pope.

"Yes?" she snarled.

"I'm really sorry to bother you again, Mrs. Farmer, but you have to come in to my office and sign Nick out. We can only release him to a parent or guardian."

"Great! Well, he'll have to wait. I'll get over there as soon as I can."

She dropped the phone in its cradle and settled into her chair. Straightening her spine, forcing herself to concentrate on her computer screen, she churned out the document Gerry needed with only moments to spare. Once she delivered the final product into his eager hands, she returned to her desk, pushed aside a pile of papers, and let her head sink onto her folded arms.

The last thing she wanted to do was head up to the school and face Nick. She hated scenes, and her son was a pro at creating them.

Hearing a soft knock on her door, she jerked her head up. Carol, her best friend and the agency's art director, pushed the door open and poked her head inside.

"Hi, there." An avid gardener like Anna, she approached the desk, a library book in her hands. "I thought you might like to look at this before I returned it. It's got a great section on keeping pests out of your garden without using poisons or insecticides."

Anna didn't even feign interest in the book. She put her head back down on her arms.

"What's the matter, sweetie? Having a bad morning? Can I help you release some of the tension?" Carol moved behind Anna and began massaging her shoulders. "A quick back rub will make you feel better."

For a few minutes, the friends remained in comfortable silence. Finally Carol spoke. "You have a pressure point right here." She dug her thumb into a particularly sore area to the left of Anna's shoulder blade.

"Ow! That hurts!"

"Good. That means I got the right spot. Now, just take it easy, and let my magic hands do their job."

Anna soon relaxed enough to tell her friend about Ms. Blackmun's calls.

"So what did Nicky do to get suspended?" Carol gently prodded.

"I don't know. I was so mad at the little shit I forgot to ask."

"I hope he didn't get caught with drugs or something awful like that."

"I don't think so. That's an automatic expulsion, isn't it? Knowing Nick, he probably went off on his Spanish teacher again. He really hates that woman. I just hope he didn't get violent."

"Oh, come on, Anna. I've known Nicky since he was in grade school. He's not the violent type."

"I don't know about that. The way he's been acting lately, I wouldn't put anything past him."

Carol's hands slowed. "He's never hurt you, has he?"

"Not physically, no."

Carol swept her hands up and down Anna's spine and then squeezed her shoulders. "Okay, I'm done. I've gotten the knots out." She settled her round derriere in a chair by the desk.

Stretching her arms over her head, Anna glanced at her friend. Instead of finding solace in Carol's kind expression, jealousy gnawed at her. It wasn't fair. Carol had a loving husband and grown twin daughters who adored her. Tracey and Ellen had probably never given their mother a moment of trouble. Anna couldn't imagine the twins treating Carol and her husband with the disrespect Nick showed her.

Anna took a deep breath, forcing her unkind thoughts out of her head. The last thing she needed now was to compromise her relationship with her best friend. "I might as well stop putting off the inevitable and go get him. I can't wait to find out what my darling son has done this time."

"I'll cover for you with Gerry. He should be in that meeting with the CEO of Footwear Unlimited until at least noon."

"I'll be back by then."

"Aye, aye, Cap'n. If ye need anything, yer matey be at yer service!" Carol rolled up a piece of paper and held the funnel to her mouth. "Launch the long boats, men," she called out.

Anna laughed, and the tension inside her released another notch. She could never stay mad when Carol was around. With her good heart and oddball sense of humor, the woman could charm the diamonds off a rattler. Carol was the only person who could give Anna advice without risking her friend's wrath, and she was a pro at rescuing Anna from her dark moods.

In the car, Anna began to worry about her son's latest screw-up. What could Nick have done to land him a week's suspension? Had he gotten into a fight or threatened a teacher the way he sometimes threatened her? Since his father had died, his behavior had steadily worsened, and she no longer trusted him. His volatility and unpredictability made him seem capable of anything.

Where had her sweet little boy gone? In elementary and middle school, Nick was an excellent student and an enthusiastic—if not particularly talented—athlete. His teachers loved him, and Anna glowed with pride over his accomplishments. However, when Kevin died, he left her with a twelve-year-old boy just entering puberty. She had known little about adolescent boys and their development, other than that they needed strong male role models—not her specialty. Since then, her son had become uncontrollable. He no longer cared about grades or what adults thought of him, and he had dropped out of sports completely. The thing she hated most about the "new" Nick was his attitude. He was ornery and antagonistic, fighting anyone he perceived to be an authority figure. Especially his mother.

To make matters worse, now that his high school had merged with a school in the rougher part of the township, he'd started hanging out with a new crowd. She didn't know any of the other parents or what morals they might be teaching their kids. God only knew what influence his peer group was having on Nick.

When Anna noticed a police car pass her on the other side of the street, she automatically slowed. The cruiser made a U-turn, and came up behind her, red and blue lights flashing. She pulled over to allow it to pass. To her astonishment, the cop car followed her to the curb. Her heart began to race. What had she done?

She rolled down the window of her ten-year-old Saab and looked up into the unlined face of an officer who looked to be in his twenties, his blue uniform shirt stretching across an already bulging belly.

"May I see your license, registration, and proof of insurance, please, ma'am?"

"Did I do something wrong, officer? I didn't go through a stop sign, did I? I'm in a rush. Maybe I missed something."

The police officer pointed to the corner of her windshield. "Your inspection sticker expired last month."

Big fucking deal, she wanted to shout at him. *Don't you have anything better to do than harass law-abiding citizens?* Instead, she bit the inside of her cheek and reached into the glove compartment for her documents. As she handed them over, she looked up at the young officer and forced a smile. "I'm a single mother with a demanding job. I'm really, really busy. Do you think you could cut me a break? Maybe just give me a warning or something?"

The oaf acted as though he hadn't heard a word she'd said. "I'll be back as soon as I run these through the computer."

Five minutes later, he returned clasping a hundred-dollar ticket in his fist. When she saw the amount of the fine, Anna slipped out of shock into anger. She bit her tongue to keep from saying something nasty to the police officer.

The final affront came when the cop said, "Have a nice day," and turned to head back to his cruiser. Unable to control herself, Anna mumbled, "Screw you, asshole."

The officer stopped in mid-stride, and Anna's heart skipped a beat. He swung around and removed his sunglasses to give her a severe look. She smiled weakly, waved, and turned the key in the ignition. The Saab roared to life. As she eased back into traffic, she forced herself to stay below the speed limit the rest of the way to Nick's school.

"Screw him! He's an asshole!" Nick exclaimed, coming out of his seat in the counselor's office.[1]

Ms. Blackmun reached for his hand. "It's okay, Nick. I understand that things have really changed around here since the kids from Lincoln came over to our campus. We're all going through a period of adjustment."

He sank back in his seat, trying to swallow his anger at the injustice of the situation. Ms. Blackmun was cool. She had always been straight with him. "It's not the new kids that are the problem. It's that jerk Thompson. He can't stand the fact that his upper middle class suburban school is being overrun by townies. He's running Shady Hill like a drill sergeant and suspending anyone who disagrees with him."

"Is that what you really, honestly believe, Nick? That the principal suspended you because you were one of the leaders of the sit-in? Why didn't any of the other kids get in trouble the way you did?"

He knew what his counselor was trying to do. She wanted him to admit that he'd been wrong to lose it when the assistant principal and the stupid gym teacher had tried to carry him out of the principal's office. Sure he'd fought them. They had no right to put their hands on him.

He glared at his counselor. "Yeah. That's what I think. He doesn't want me in this school because I paid attention in Social Studies class last year when we learned about Martin Luther King and civil disobedience."

He could tell by her surprised look that Ms. Blackmun hadn't seen that one coming. Nick sat up straighter and puffed out his chest. Despite his anger at the principal for suspending him, he still felt buzzed about the success of the sit-in he'd helped organize. By storming into his office and taking over, they had really shocked Thompson. Maybe he'd think twice before inviting the cops back to Shady Hill to break into lockers and violate the students' civil rights.

Ms. Blackmun pinned him with a stern look. "Did any teacher ever tell you that Dr. King or Mahatma Gandhi kicked, bit or swore at an arresting officer?"

Nick's eyes dropped to the floor, and he slumped back into his chair. Ms. Blackmun had a point. He shouldn't have lost control when they tried to evict him from Thompson's office. His mother always warned him that his mouth would get him into trouble if he didn't learn to turn it off. Still, what he had done was nothing compared to what the adults were doing to his school.

Since he couldn't figure out how to talk his way out of admitting he'd made a mistake, Nick clammed up. No point digging himself into an even deeper hole.

There was a sharp rap on the door. His whole body tensed in preparation for his mother's grand entrance. Now the crap would really hit the fan.

"Here's the lunch you ordered, Sylvia," a woman's raspy voice announced. Nick looked up, relief flooding through him at the sight of the middle-aged hall monitor who entered the small office and put a tray on the desk.

"Thank you, Nancy."

Once the woman left, Ms. Blackmun pushed the tray toward Nick. "Help me eat this?" she asked. Two cartons of chocolate milk, a tuna hoagie, chips, and a side salad sat on the tray.

Surprised, Nick looked up at his small, wiry counselor. "You eat all this for lunch?"

She laughed. "I have a good metabolism. Now let's eat."

Anna arrived at the high school, her head pounding and her nerves shot. Work deadlines, the cost of a hundred-dollar ticket she couldn't afford plus the expense of getting her car inspected, and another embarrassing trip to bail Nick out of trouble weighed heavily on her heart. She didn't know how much more she could take.

Once inside the expansive two-story brick building, Anna found the girls' room. She needed a few minutes to get herself together before facing her son and his advisor. Leaning over the sink to check her makeup, she overheard two students talking between stalls.

"I think what the cops did was really screwed up. They shouldn't have opened those kids' lockers without their permission," one girl stated. "Isn't that illegal?"

"I don't know why you're so upset. It's not like any of our friends got caught. The cops only picked on the new kids from Lincoln."

"Yeah, but what if they bring in drug-sniffing dogs next time? What if one of them smells weed on me?"

Her friend laughed. "If you're so worried about it, then stop smoking pot with Jason in the parking lot every morning before homeroom."

A toilet flushed. Quickly, so the girls wouldn't think she'd been eavesdropping, Anna slipped out the door. From the little she'd heard, she had a pretty strong suspicion that Nick had challenged the authorities during the police raid. He was always railing against the system, as if any one person could really change the status quo. If, as the girls said, the cops had targeted only the new kids from Lincoln, then her brilliant son had probably gotten himself in trouble by defending one of his loser friends from across town.

When Anna walked into the administrative suite, the secretary at the front desk waved her through. She approached Ms. Blackmun's office and took a deep breath before knocking.

"Come in," a voice called out.

Anna opened the door and poked her head in. The school counselor, who was in her mid- to late-twenties, sat at her desk sharing a tray of cafeteria food with Nick. The cozy scene brought home to Anna that her only child could still charm the pants off adults when it suited him.

If only he would stop fighting her and settle down, their lives would be so much simpler. The direction Nick was headed, he wouldn't make it through high school, let alone college. And he needed a college education to become a professional and avoid the trap she had gotten herself into—working at a menial job she hated for a paycheck she desperately needed. He had to start listening to her before it was too late.

When he craned his neck to look at her, she asked, "So, Nick, what's going on?" Remembering what Dr. Elliot, the psychologist Nick had seen several times, had told her about building trust by withholding judgment, she tried not to jump down her son's throat. Instead, she forced a smile and went for a touch of humor. "What am I bailing you out for this time?"

Nick threw his half-eaten hoagie down, his hostile glare spearing her with its fierceness. "Jesus Christ. Can't you, just once, cut me a break? Why don't you trust me? You always think I'm guilty of some terrible crime before you hear my side of the story. God, I hate you!²

He stood up, his fists clenched at his sides.

The counselor rose from her chair. She grabbed his forearm. "Hey, Nick. You've had an upsetting morning. Why don't you sit down and tell your mom what happened?"

Nick turned to Ms. Blackmun, who was gazing warmly at him. He slumped back into his chair, his long, skinny legs sprawled out in front of him and his arms crossed over his chest.

Anna took the seat the counselor indicated and waited. Nick stared at her. Mixed in with his defiant I-dare-you-to-say-anything look, she caught a glimpse of the insecure little boy who still wanted her approval. Somewhat reassured, she waited to hear what he had to say.

"The cops were here this morning. Our brilliant principal, who thinks he's running a prison camp, invited them in to check for drugs. It was bad enough that the cops invaded our privacy by forcing open lockers, but then Thompson had the nerve to expel a bunch of kids from Lincoln on the spot. They'd only been here a month, but he didn't even give them a warning."

So, Anna thought, her assumption had been correct. Nick was all bent out of shape about the police action because some of his new friends had been kicked out.

A tremendous wave of guilt rolled over Anna. This was all her fault. She had let her son hang out with the wrong crowd. Now he would be labeled a troublemaker for the rest of his time at this school. He'd never get into a decent college.[3]

She turned to her son, who was studying a framed diploma on the wall. "Look at me, Nick." He reluctantly turned in her direction, his eyes filled with defiant anger. What did he have to be pissed about? She was the one who should be furious. "Were *you* searched? Those 'supposed' friends you've been hanging out with, they were the ones who got expelled, weren't they?" She heard her voice rising in decibels, the accusations she had tried to staunch flowing freely now. "How many times have I told you to stay away from that crowd, that they would bring you down?"

This time Ms. Blackmun wasn't fast enough to grab him. Nick bounded from his chair and bolted for the door.

The counselor jumped to her feet. "You can't leave school grounds until your mother and I are finished here. Come on, Nick. Don't get yourself in any more trouble."

"Fuck you!" he shouted. He threw open the door and ran out. The door slammed against the wall, then swung back.[4]

Anna looked at the counselor. Shaken, she asked, "What did I say that was so bad? What did I do wrong?"

Ms. Blackmun's calm countenance had disappeared. Her face flushed, she tapped nervously with her pencil on her desk calendar. "I'm not sure exactly what set him off, but your son is very sensitive to anything that might be construed as an injustice. I think he felt you falsely accused him and his friends of something they didn't do."

Anna cleared her throat. "But I was right, wasn't I? Some of the students who were expelled had to be his buddies."

"I don't think so. If they were, Nick never mentioned it to me. He's a smart kid, Mrs. Farmer. He's quite capable of seeing the larger picture. I think he got upset about the police search-and-seizure operation this morning for exactly the reason he told you. He felt the police unfairly targeted the new kids and violated their right to privacy."

What? If Nick and his friends hadn't been affected by the police operation, then why was her son in trouble?

Ms. Blackmun answered the question before Anna could ask. "Nick helped organize a student sit-in at the principal's office. When the kids were asked to leave, the other students went peacefully, but your son refused to go. The vice-principal and the sports director had to forcibly remove him. He gave them quite a fight and slung more than a few choice words at them." She shrugged her shoulders. "Frankly, I think Nick handled himself admirably until that final altercation. He wasn't afraid of voicing his opinion, and he had some valid points. However, after it was all over, Mr. Thompson had no choice but to suspend him."

Anna couldn't believe her ears. This bubble-brained school counselor actually felt empathy for Nick. Obviously too close to her own teen years, the young thing failed to see how damaging Nick's anti-authoritarian behaviors could be to his future. It wouldn't have been so bad if he had just gone along with the other protesters, but Nick always had to be different, more out there than his peers.[5]

As usual, her son had only been thinking of himself and his high and mighty principles. He hadn't thought for even a microsecond about her or her reputation in the community. What if people at work caught wind of his suspension? They'd blame her and talk about her behind her back. They'd say she was a failure as a mother.[6]

The harsh beeping of her cell phone interrupted Anna's thoughts. She checked the caller ID and frowned.

"Excuse me a minute. My office is on the line."

Luckily, she took Carol's call sitting down.

"May Day. May Day. Get back here quick, Cap'n. All hell's broken loose. Upland Petroleum wants its ad campaign completely revamped by Friday. This Friday. As in four working days from today."

"I'll be there in twenty minutes." Anna snapped the phone shut. "I need to get going. You said you had papers for me to sign?"

"But—"

Before the counselor could give her a hard time about Nick's absence, Anna gave the young woman her steeliest glare and added, "I'm sure Nick hasn't left the campus. He's too lazy to walk home. He's probably waiting by the car for me."

The counselor handed over the documents. Once everything was settled, Anna said goodbye and headed for the parking lot.

Nick leaned against the dented fender of the Saab, trying to look like he was chilling in the parking lot during his lunch period instead of waiting for his mother to take him home. He knew he'd been given a raw deal and shouldn't care, but the suspension still stung. His freshman year he had been in trouble a couple of times, but he and Ms.

Blackmun had always worked stuff out. This year was shaping up to be different. He hated most of his teachers, especially Mrs. Johnson, the witch who taught his first period Spanish class, and the principal was acting like an uptight asshole, hiring a bunch of new hall monitors to make life tough for the students.

Since he and his girlfriend Kelly didn't share any free periods this semester, they usually hooked up between classes. One of the new monitors had written them up three times in the last week for being late to class, which was bullshit. He had to see Kelly during school or he'd die, and it wasn't like they missed anything important in the first minute or two of class.

He thought about pulling out a cigarette and lighting up. Hell, he was already suspended from school. What could the Gestapo do to him if they caught him? He glanced nervously at the door his mother would come through any second, and his craving disappeared. The last thing he needed was a lecture from the Goddess of Perfection on the dangers of smoking.

As he predicted, the door opened and his mother's slim figure appeared silhouetted in the doorway. She paused to check that he was at the car, then descended the wide stone steps, heading toward him. His heart began to pound in anticipation of the argument to come. His mother was bad enough in public. When they were alone, she liked to really dig her claws into him.

"Hey, Nick! How did you get out of class?"

His face burned with embarrassment. Turning, he watched Kelly step out of her friend's car, a Coke from McDonald's gripped in one hand, several books balanced in the crook of her other arm.

"I got screwed by Thompson. The asshole suspended me for a week for organizing the sit-in," he informed her.

The concerned look on his girlfriend's face wiped away all Nick's negative thoughts. Kelly was so cool. She was the only person in the whole world who really understood him. He heard the click of his mother's shoes on the pavement, then the jingle of her keys as she unlocked the car door. His attention remained riveted on Kelly.

The driver's side door opened. "Come on, Nick. Get in. I have an emergency at work."

Kelly sidled up to him. He leaned over and kissed her on the mouth. When she responded to him, his arm automatically draped around her shoulders. He pulled her closer.

Deeply engrossed in the kiss, he didn't notice his mother tapping on the car windshield. A sudden, loud honk from the Saab jolted him out of his trance. Jumping back, he let go of Kelly, who, thrown off balance, dropped her stack of books and soda.

The horn beeped again. Nick turned long enough to glare at his mother, then bent down to pick up Kelly's things. "Sorry about that, Kel. Mom's having a hissy fit, as usual. Call me after school, and I'll tell you everything that happened."

"Okay."

Her smile made him feel warm all over. He pressed a quick kiss on her cheek and opened the car door.

Wide-eyed, Anna stared at her son. She had no idea Nick had been dating, or that he had a girlfriend. For a moment, she forgot her anger, a pang of sadness taking its place. Her son hadn't confided in her in a long time. They had drifted so far apart that Anna had stopped asking him anything about his personal life, knowing he would stonewall her.[7]

Nick dumped his lanky body into the passenger's seat. Closing the door, he rolled down his window. Before he could start up again with the girl, Anna threw the car into gear and pulled out of the parking lot.

Now that she had Nick as a captive audience, she ought to discuss the day's events with him, but she didn't think she had the strength for yet another confrontation. Despite Dr. Elliot's admonishment to keep out of Nick's teenage dramas, more often than not she couldn't stop herself. Better to wait until this evening when she could talk rationally with Nick about what had happened. "I'll try to get home early for dinner tonight. We can discuss what happened then. Okay?"

Instead of answering her, Nick reached out and turned on the radio, immediately flipping from her favorite soft rock station to his favorite hip-hop station. Anna hated rap, and he knew it. As if he could read her mind, Nick did exactly what she hoped he wouldn't. He turned up the volume until the bass made the old car shake and her head pound.

Swerving off the road, she slammed on the brakes and threw the car into neutral. Reaching over, she shut off the radio and turned to Nick. "That's it. I've had enough of your disrespect. You're grounded for the rest of the semester, buddy."

Acting as if he hadn't heard her, Nick leaned over and turned the radio on again.

Anna slapped his hand away and snapped the music off. Twisting in her seat, she shouted in his face, "When are you going to grow up and think about someone else besides yourself? You are a selfish, insensitive brat. I'm embarrassed to call you my son."[8]

"That is it! That is really it!" Nick threw his door open and clambered out of the car. When he reached in to grab his backpack, Anna saw tears glinting in his eyes. A pang of remorse shot through her, and her anger dissipated as quickly as it had erupted.

She leaned over the gearshift, trying to get his attention. "Come on, Nick. I'm sorry. Get in the car and quit acting like a baby—"

He slammed the door in her face and took off, striding purposefully down the street. Anna put the car in first gear and followed along the shoulder. Leaning across the empty seat, she called to him through the open window. "Please, Nick. I'm in a hurry. Get in."

He ignored her, turning his face away from her. Her hazard lights blinking, she followed him for several blocks. Torn between her responsibilities at the office and her duty to keep Nick safe, she made one last attempt to get him to back down, but he kept walking.

Anna sighed in frustration. Turning off the hazard lights, she moved cautiously into the traffic lane. They were less than a mile from home and Nick knew the way. He'd have to get there on his own. She couldn't afford to be fired from her job.

Half a block away, she checked her rearview mirror and saw him standing in the dirt at the side of the road, watching her go. Instinctively, she put her hand up and waved. When he gave her a tentative wave in return, her heart sank to the pit of her stomach. Feeling like the world's worst mother but not knowing what else to do, she drove away.

As soon as the Saab turned the corner, Nick wiped his eyes with the sleeve of his shirt, cursing himself. He always felt bad after fighting with his mother. Why couldn't he be strong and tell her to fuck off and really mean it? She had been a bitch today, making him feel like a dog who had pissed on the new carpet, but he had still waved to her and acted like he had forgiven her. Maybe he had. A part of him understood that she missed Dad as much as he did. He knew she worked for a jerk like Gerry because she had to, not because she wanted to. Nick hated to admit it, but he kind of missed the days when his mother hadn't worked and they had been close, although there was no way he wanted to go back there. Too much had changed. *He* had changed.[9]

Nick kicked up a cloud of dust from the dirt along the roadside. Okay, so he *had* tried to piss his mother off by turning the radio up, but that didn't give her the right to go off on him and tell him he embarrassed her. She was his mom, and not once had she asked him how he felt about getting suspended. Today had been one of the worst days of his life, but his mother had expressed zero sympathy for him.

She thought he was selfish, but what about her? She was the one who worried about other people blaming her for his behaviors, as if he did shit just to punish her. Hell, teenagers were supposed to give their parents a hard time. His mom should chill and let him do his own thing instead of being constantly on his case. Maybe then they could live together under the same roof without killing each other.

In an act of defiance that he knew his mother would never see, Nick stopped, pulled a cigarette out of his backpack, and lit it with the lighter Kelly had given him. Taking a deep drag, he held the smoke in his lungs until the nicotine kicked in, and he felt better. Dragging on his cigarette, he took his time walking the rest of the way home, his thoughts turning to more important matters—like how soon he and Kelly could be alone again.

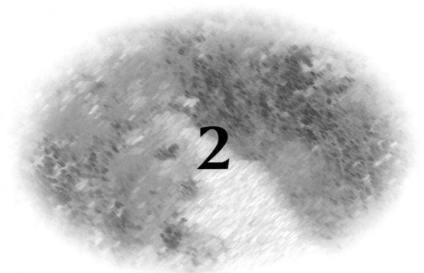

2

Anna returned to an office in chaos. All afternoon her ear stayed glued to the telephone. When she wasn't talking to officials at the oil company, she was faxing or sending messengers to their corporate offices with the latest in a stream of proposals and storyboards cranked out by her ad agency's creative department.

At six-thirty, with final approval for the new campaign only a matter of the wording in the contract, Gerry gave the copywriting and design shops the okay to close up for the night.

Relieved that the rush was over, Anna packed her briefcase with the most urgent papers she needed to attend to before the next business day. She would plow through them at home after she'd talked to Nick.

"Where do you think you're going?" a male voice demanded.

She spun around. Her boss, his handlebar moustache waxed into fine points at the ends, filled her office doorway with his bulk.

"My house, Gerry. I promised Nick I'd have dinner with him."

"No way, José. I need you here when the contract arrives from Upland. You're my business manager. You're the one who negotiated the terms of the agreement. I'll be in my office. When you're sure what's on paper is what we agreed to, bring it in, and I'll sign."

"But Gerry. Nick—"

"You heard what I said, Anna." Her boss let out a nasal laugh. "Believe me, Nick won't lose any sleep over missing a chance to chat with you. When my sons were teenagers, they didn't want to have anything to do with their mother. Leave the poor kid alone."

Gerry's words stung. He had never been a single parent. He didn't understand how guilt ate her up when she had to work late and leave Nick alone. On more than one occasion, her son had accused her of choosing her job over him. He was right. She was trapped on the money treadmill. Without the salary Gerry paid her, which was the best she could hope for without a college degree, she and Nick would be out on the street.[10]

Anna had never been good at facing down her intimidating boss, and she didn't plan to do so tonight. Instead, she averted her gaze and waited. Once she heard his heavy steps recede down the hallway, she reached for the phone and dialed home. Nick picked up after the first ring.

"Hi, hon. I'm stuck at work waiting for a delivery. I'll be a little late."

"How late is late?"

"I don't know. It depends on when the papers get here."

"Do you think you'll be home in, say, half an hour?"

It had been a long, hard day. Nick's persistence irritated Anna, and she couldn't keep the annoyance out of her voice. "Why? What are you up to? You can't go out, you know. You're grounded."

"Never mind," Nick spat into the phone before killing the connection.

Anna slowly replaced the receiver. She couldn't help thinking that modern society, with its strict child abuse laws, had it all wrong. Maybe keeping kids on a tight leash and beating the hell out of them if they disobeyed wasn't a bad parenting strategy after all.[11]

Leaning over, she slipped off her shoes, grabbed her right foot, and began to massage her instep through her stockings. Her mood had sunk to a new low—somewhere between too-exhausted-to-think and totally pissed. Her stomach growled, and she rubbed it.

"Quite a day, eh, Cap'n?" Carol's cheerful voice floated into the office from the hallway.

Anna breathed a sigh of relief. She needed to vent to someone she could trust, and Carol was a great listener.

"Boy, am I glad to see you. Come in and take a load off. I'll fill you in on what's happening with Nick."

To her surprise, Carol shook her head. "I promised Ellen I'd go to the school board meeting tonight. They're introducing the new teachers in the system to the community." Her friend beamed proudly.

"That's right. I forgot she started teaching kindergarten this fall."

"Why don't you come, too, Anna? I'll tell Frank to meet us there. You can drop your car off at home, and I'll drive you to the meeting. On the way, you can tell me all the latest."

Anna looked at Carol helplessly. "I'd love to, but Gerry won't let me out of here until the new contract is signed. The papers haven't arrived yet."

The office doorbell rang. Carol glanced at her watch. "That must be the delivery service. How long will it take you to proof the contract? I could wait for you."

"If it isn't screwed up, which it probably will be, about ten minutes."

"Come on, Anna. Try being optimistic for a change. Things might work out better if you were."

"Thank you, Dr. Freud." Anna rose from her chair, but her friend motioned her back.

"Relax. I'll get the package."

Outside the house, a car horn blared.

"Shit!" Nick's gut tightened. His ride to the school board meeting had arrived, and he hadn't called his mother back to explain what he planned to do. When she'd called earlier, he had been too pissed at her to tell her that the senior class president had called and asked him *as a personal favor* to speak at the meeting. He might have turned Allison down if his mom had come home on time. To try and smooth things over between them, he had cooked her a spaghetti dinner as a surprise. But everything was ruined now, so there was really no point in waiting around. He knew she'd go ballistic when she realized he had defied her, but he'd deal with that later.

He turned off the oven and grabbed his coat. Making sure the key to the house was in his pocket, he let himself out the front door.

"Hey, Nick!" Allison waved to him from the driver's seat of her VW Passat. He opened the back door and hesitated, not knowing what to do since every seat was already taken.

"Come on, guys. Squeeze over, or Nick'll have to sit on someone's lap."

"He can sit on mine!" said a tiny girl with a high voice, the person closest to the open door.

Allison laughed. "I think it better be the other way around, Squeak. Get out and let Nick sit down, and then you scoot onto his lap. Okay?"

Nick turned red with embarrassment at the thought of having a strange girl perched on his knees, but he did as Allison requested. Before the overloaded car had pulled out of his driveway, the girl named Squeak began to talk to him. "I think what you did at school today was way cool. You really showed that asshole Thompson. I wish I'd had the courage to do what you did."

His cheeks burned, and this time not from embarrassment. "Thanks," he said, trying to sound as if he didn't care. "I saw right away that he was targeting the new kids, and that's not fair. Our school had plenty of problems last year. It's not as if the kids from Lincoln had anything to do with that."

"Exactly," Allison shot back. "You should bring that up at the meeting, Nick. Someone needs to point out how prejudicial the raid was to the Lincoln students. I looked up the law on search-and-seizure raids in public schools. I plan to argue the legality of what the police and Principal Thompson did. In at least one case, I believe they overstepped their authority."

Nick wasn't quite sure what Allison had said, but he knew what he had to do. For the rest of the short trip to the administration building, he and the other students discussed the best way to present their case to the school board. By the time they arrived and took seats in the rear of the auditorium, he felt as though he had become part of something important, something that could make things better for all the students at Shady Hill. His worries about his mother's reaction when she found out he'd broken his grounding completely vanished. Once she knew he had the smartest girl in the high school supporting his cause, she'd see that he'd been right, and she'd be proud of him.

Anna tried calling Nick to tell him she might be going to the school board meeting, but he didn't answer. To hell with him, she thought, taking the package from Carol's hand and ripping it open. If he didn't have the decency to pick up the phone, then she wouldn't worry about leaving him home alone tonight.

In less than fifteen minutes, she had proofed the final documents and handed them over to Gerry. When she dropped her car off at home, she popped her head into the suspiciously darkened house and called Nick's name. He didn't answer, and she didn't hear the TV going or the sound of an electronic game playing. Her concern for her son turned to anger. It looked like he had flown the coop. She had no clue what he thought he was accomplishing by disobeying her so blatantly, other than starting World War Three.

Her thoughts in turmoil, she hopped into Carol's van and began to vent. By the time they arrived at the meeting, she had released some of her anger, but still felt hurt and abused by Nick's total disregard for her.

Ellen had reserved a seat for her mother close to the front of the auditorium, which was more than half full. Her family members and friends moved over to make room for Anna.

School Board President Harry Gruber, who owned the local car dealership where Anna had bought her Saab, banged his gavel, trying to call the noisy crowd to order. The loudspeaker crackled, and his magnified voice bellowed, "Please, folks. This is not a gabfest. We need to get started. The first item on the agenda is old business."

Harry methodically called each item on the list. Different administrators or board members gave boring reports. Anna had to keep pinching herself to stay awake.

The last piece of old business was a report by the school district's facilities manager about the successful integration of Lincoln High School into Shady Hill. The audience, up until now expressing as much enthusiasm for the proceedings as Anna, suddenly came alive. The bitter debate over the merger was still fresh in residents' minds. The consolidation had staved off a huge tax increase but had caused much animosity and ill will between the segments of the community forced to adjust to the changes.

The manager finished his glowing report amidst a growing rumbling in the crowd. When a parent tried to use the microphone set up for audience participation, the board president cut him off. "I'm sorry, but the report was simply that. A report. The chair is not taking any questions from the floor about old business. We've discussed the consolidation of the two schools ad nauseum for two years. There's nothing more to be said on the subject.

"Now, on to new business. I've invited Principal Thompson of Shady Hill and Police Chief Marshall to speak to you about the search-and-seizure program we've initiated in the senior high school."

The two men arose from their seats in the front row and climbed the stairs to the stage. The crowd buzzed with anticipation. Most had come to the meeting to voice their opinions about the raid.

Heads turned as a group of students who had been sitting in the shadows at the rear of the auditorium moved en masse toward the microphone.

Anna twisted in her seat. Her mouth fell open. At the forefront of the group of young rebels strode Nick, a cocky grin on his face. She felt her face grow hot. Knowing she had to stop him, Anna began to rise from her chair.

Carol grabbed her arm and pulled her back. "Let him do his thing."

Anna turned on Carol. "Let him stand there and make a fool out of me?" she asked, stunned at her friend's lack of support.

Shaking her head, Carol whispered, "How is Nick making a fool out of you, Anna? This whole thing isn't about you. The board needs input from the students. Nick might have something important to say that they need to hear."[12]

Anna had never been so offended in her life. Carol had betrayed her. Her face tingling, she grabbed her handbag. "I'm out of here."

"Come on, honey," Carol said, softly but with force. "Don't leave. Stay and see what happens."

Hunched over so as not to draw attention to herself, Anna inched in front of the seats in her row until she reached the aisle. She had to get out of here before Nick stood in front of the microphone and identified himself as her son.

Her head down, she scurried up the side aisle to the back door.[13] When she exited the building, the chilly night air hit her full in the face, but it didn't cool her off. She sat on the cement steps letting hot tears fall. Carol's ridiculous words rang in her ears. *This isn't about you, Anna.* Of course it was about her. She'd raised Nick, hadn't she? And during his difficult early teen years, she'd done it alone. If his actions didn't reflect on her, then on whom did they reflect? God?

Carol would probably say that Nick was expressing himself and that was supposed to make the stupid things he did—like piercing his ears and wearing those ridiculous baggy pants around his knees—okay. Well, they weren't okay. Not as long as she was his parent.[14]

Anna heard angry shouts coming from inside the building and shuddered. She was tempted to reenter the hall to find out what was happening, but vetoed the idea. She was too upset. She didn't need to know that Nick was in trouble again.

She tried to keep herself together by telling herself she was being overly dramatic. She'd had a bad day. A really bad day. Things seemed bleak, but maybe they'd be better in the morning. Maybe. If Nick and his friends weren't causing a riot at the school board meeting.

Finding a paper napkin in her purse, Anna blew her nose, dried her eyes, and waited. The noise gradually died down inside the administration building until all she could hear was the whoosh of cars speeding by on the highway across from the parking lot. No police cruisers appeared. After fifteen minutes, she relaxed. It didn't look like she'd have to go bail her son out of jail tonight after all.

She was sitting in the shadows leaning against a fluted column when the students burst through the swinging doors.

"Awesome, dude," she heard one boy say as he slapped Nick on the back. The group of a dozen or so moved as one unit toward the parking lot.

"You know, Nick, you should run for student council next year. That was some speech," the girl in the lead called over her shoulder.

In seconds, they were gone, leaving Anna alone on the steps with a vague sense of guilt and a curiosity that had to be satisfied. She slipped back into the hall in time to see the new teachers acknowledged and the meeting adjourned.

Carol and her family came down the aisle together. When she saw Anna, her friend broke away from the group.

Anna impatiently grabbed Carol's forearm. "What happened? What did Nick do?"

Carol slipped her arm around Anna's waist and guided them toward her van.

"That had to be one of the wildest school board meetings I've ever seen. The kids were great. Do you know Allison Lyons? She's a senior, president of her class, headed for Yale like her father, no doubt, and eventually a brilliant career in law. She researched the whole search-and-seizure phenomenon and discovered that, at least in one case, the cops and the school district didn't follow proper procedures. Apparently, they opened a boy's locker when he wasn't present and without just cause, which was a violation of his rights."

Anna was interested in the meeting's outcome, but she couldn't stand waiting to hear about her son. "So, what about Nick? What did he say?"

Carol's eyes rolled in her head. "That kid should be a labor mediator or a social worker when he grows up. After Allison's speech, the parents started taking sides, pretty much along the lines you would expect—former Lincoln families versus Shady Hill families. The Lincoln folks wanted the school board to launch an investigation of the superintendent and the police chief. The Shady Hill contingent wanted to give the authorities a medal for smoking out the lowlife drug dealers that had invaded their school. There was a lot of shouting, and I think a scuffle would have broken out if Nick hadn't taken over the mike."

"And?" Anna could barely breathe.

"He asked the school board what they planned to do to help the kids they had just expelled. He gave a very impassioned speech about the divisions in the high school and how the administration is targeting the new kids because they're from the less affluent side of town. He challenged the parents from the 'right' side of town who thought their kids were so honorable and well-behaved to go home and ask them if they had ever smoked weed or gotten drunk at parties or if they'd ever cheated on a test. He assured them their kids were doing all those things long before the 'bad' element arrived at Shady Hill."

Carol paused, chuckling. "Yessiree. Young Nick certainly gave them a piece of his mind. It shut those self-righteous, bigoted parents right up."

Carol unlocked the van and they got in. Anna sat in stunned silence while her friend drove her home. She had never thought of Nick as someone capable of mature adult behavior. At home, he acted like a two-year-old.[15] Remembering the nasty tone of their recent arguments, she asked suspiciously, "Did he use the 'F' word in public?"

"Come on, Anna. Let it go. Your son did great. He may be a pain in the ass to you, but he has a lot going for him. You need to let yourself see his good side and not get so stuck in the crap he throws at you."

Anna slumped in her seat. "I don't understand him. He was such a sweet child before Kevin..." Her voice trailed off. Tears welling in her eyes, she looked over at her friend. "He's too much for me. I can't handle him by myself."

Carol shook her head and made a tsking sound. "Sure you can. You love him, and even though it seems like he doesn't love you most of the time, he does."

Anna put her head in her hands. "I really screwed up tonight."

Carol didn't refute her statement, but squeezed her hand. They drove on in silence until they reached Anna's comfortable colonial.

"Want to come in for a few minutes?"

Carol glanced at her watch. "Okay, but I can't stay long."

Anna tried the front door, disappointed to find it still locked because that meant that Nick wasn't home yet. Once she had the door open, she guided Carol into the living room. Nick never used the room, and it was the only one in the house she was relatively certain to find clean.

Anna sat on the couch, offering her friend the comfortable recliner. She noticed the light flashing on her answering machine. "Mind if I listen to my messages? Nick may have left word about when he'll be home."

Carol shrugged. "Be my guest."

Anna leaned over and hit the play button.

"Hi, Mom. It's me. I'm spending the night at Bob's house. His mother will drive me home in the morning on her way to work."

Anna vaguely remembered a boy with curly brown hair and a nose ring that Nick had introduced her to in September. Bob was one of her son's new friends from the other side of town.

She snapped the machine off. "I don't believe it. Just when I'm starting to feel good about the kid, he goes and does something like this. I can't let him sleep out after all the rules he's broken today. That would be rewarding bad behavior." She put on her reading glasses so she could decipher the numbers on the caller ID screen. "I guess I should call to get the address and then go pick Nick up."

Carol put a steadying hand over Anna's. "At least he called. That shows he doesn't want you to worry about him." She paused for a moment, then added, "Maybe it's better for Nicky to sleep over at his friend's house tonight. You two could probably use some time apart."

Anna usually didn't like getting unsolicited advice from her friends, but in this instance, Carol was probably right. She was tired and confused. Frankly, she didn't feel strong enough to face her son this evening.

They talked for a few more minutes, then Anna accompanied her friend to the front door.

Carol brushed a kiss across her cheek. "You get a good night's sleep, honey, and I'll see you at work in the morning."

Anna watched the older woman walk down the driveway. Carol had almost reached her car when she turned and added, "Remember, it's always darkest before the dawn. You'll see. Things will start looking up soon."

Anna wanted to believe her optimistic friend, but she couldn't. The situation with Nick was too confusing. The sessions with Dr. Elliot had helped some, but not enough. Something had to give or she would lose her son for good.

She couldn't change what had already gone on between them, and she was beginning to think she couldn't do anything to change Nick, but she could do something to help herself become a better parent.

Feeling tired but determined, she went to her home office and began sifting through the notes she had taken following Nick's sessions with Dr. Elliot, when the psychologist had discussed her son with her. She carefully studied her scribbles, growing increasingly despondent as she read. *Try not to be drawn into Nick's dramas. Take the time to understand why his actions press your buttons before you lash out or punish him.* She had failed in every way today. Nick may have screwed up, but so had she.[16]

Anna put her notes away and headed for the kitchen to make herself a cup of soothing chamomile tea. The sight of the kitchen table set for two with a clean tablecloth and matching napkins stopped her cold. Around the room, she spied the remnants of dinner. A pot of hardened spaghetti and a frying pan filled with congealed meat sauce on the stove. A loaf of toasted Italian bread sitting in a nest of tinfoil on the counter. A wilting salad dumped into the sink.

Anna's legs wobbled. She pulled a chair out and sat down. Her eyes welled up with tears. She had let her son down repeatedly today, and yet he had still tried to make a nice dinner for her, reminding her that he could be sensitive, caring, and sweet when he put his mind to it.

Too tired to think, let alone deal with her own inadequacies, Anna turned and walked from the room. With the burden of her unfulfilled life weighing heavily on her shoulders, she trudged up the stairs to the second floor, stripped off her clothes, and crawled into bed.

Nick lay on the floor beside Bob's bed and tried to go to sleep, but, after the day he'd had, he couldn't turn his brain off.

He couldn't believe how cool Bob's parents were. They let their son have a TV in his room, they never checked up on him to see if he was still awake at night, they didn't nag him about how much of a mess his room was, and his mother even seemed to like the dye job that had turned his brown hair blue.

Of course, Bob's parents didn't need to bug him to do his homework because he liked school and was getting good grades.

Nick could imagine how upset his mother would be when she got the message he'd left on the answering machine that he was sleeping over at Bob's. Even on normal days, she yelled at him for not asking her permission to do things with his friends, like he was some kind of baby or something. Seeing as how he'd gotten in so much trouble at school today and she'd tried to ground him, she'd really go postal tonight.

But he was too hurt, angry, and confused to care about her feelings. Sure, yelling at her, defying her, and saying hurtful things was making things worse between them, but she wasn't giving him any space. She was trying to control him when she should be letting him lead his own life. Trying to become a man was hard enough without his mother second-guessing him and undercutting him all the time.

Sometimes he wished he could sit down and talk to her the way he used to, but if he told his mom how screwed up he felt, she'd try to fix things for him or tell him what to do, and that would only make matters worse.[17] He wasn't trying to hurt her. He was just doing what all teenagers had to do to grow up.

3

At five the next morning, with the rising sun coloring the eastern horizon gold and red and pink, Anna dragged herself out of bed. Her sleep had been fitful at best, and although she didn't have to get up for another hour-and-a-half, she knew there would be no more rest for her.

She threw on her walking shoes, her blue sweat pants, and a long-sleeved shirt. Tying a bandanna around her head to keep her hair off her face, she headed out the door, hoping to walk off some of her depression.

After completing her first half-mile loop of the housing development, she picked up her pace. With fresh air in her lungs and her feet sounding a steady rhythm on the pavement, she felt better. On a whim, she turned into the park. This early in the morning she usually stayed off the dirt paths that meandered through the wooded acreage. There hadn't been any incidents recently, but a woman alone was always in jeopardy. Today, however, the changing leaves of autumn and majestic silence of the old growth forest beckoned to her, and she decided to take the risk.

Once inside the wrought iron gates, the pathway sloped steeply downward for several hundred feet. Tree roots, rock outcroppings, and an occasional fallen tree hampered her progress somewhat, but when the trail leveled off, she continued her brisk pace. She felt exhilarated, free, unencumbered by her failures at home and burdens at work.

Surrounded by the intense physical beauty of the Indian summer morning, she didn't worry about time or pay attention to where she was headed. Yet she felt completely safe, embraced by the wild and verdant landscape and in harmony with the small forest animals that tittered and sang in the fresh morning air.

The sound of running water caught her by surprise. She hadn't realized a stream flowed through the large tract of public land. Turning a sharp corner, she brought herself up short. A small but rapidly flowing brook twisted across her path. She didn't move, the gentle bubbling water casting a spell on her.

"Are you lost?"

She sucked in a sharp breath and took a step back. Her eyes probed the shadows. Across the stream, not more than five yards from where she stood, a dark-haired boy sat cross-legged on a flat rock facing her. As she stared at him, the sun rose another notch in the sky, bathing his half-naked body in amber light.

He looked ethereal, sitting absolutely still, his hands resting on his knees, palms up, back straight, heavy hair falling behind his bare shoulders. The unusual green stone and metal necklace around his neck caught the sun's rays and shimmered in the light. Although there was a crispness in the fall air, he seemed oblivious to the chill. His eyes were closed, but a slight smile curved his lips.

Anna looked away, embarrassed, feeling as if she had stumbled into the boy's private world. Ignoring his question, she pivoted, meaning to retrace her steps until she reached more familiar, safe ground.

"Would you like me to help you find the path?"

His youthful voice sent shivers across her shoulders and down her spine. She spun around, intending to politely reject his offer and be on her way. However, his amber eyes were open now, and when they connected with hers, they ignited something inside her. She didn't run away, the burden of her aloneness suddenly crystal clear to her. He was right. She *was* lost, figuratively as well as physically. She could no longer discern which path to take through the minefield of her life.

The boy, a total stranger, smiled at her like he was truly glad to see her, and a feeling of acceptance washed over her. Although the teen appeared to be about the same age as her son, Nick only looked at her these days with contempt in his expression.

"Come on over," the boy urged in a quiet voice that seemed to float on the wind, destined for her ears only.

She nodded, eager to close the gap between them. Keeping careful watch on her footing, she forded the stream by gingerly stepping across the moss-covered rocks. Once on firm ground again, she looked up. The boy had thrown on a white T-shirt. Standing, his baggy jeans hanging low on his hips the way Nick wore his, he helped her up onto the rock. Feeling the power of rushing water beneath her feet, she realized the stone slab jutted out across part of the stream, forming a cave beneath them.

The teenager sank gracefully into a cross-legged pose, indicating a spot for her across from him. Anna relaxed into the slight indent in the rock, surprised to find it warm to the touch. Her legs folded under her, she found his eyes again. "I have a son about your age. He's fifteen, and we don't get along at all."

She had no idea why the young man put her so at ease, but he did. An ageless, almost magical, quality shone from his eyes, which he never took off her. He smiled at her so genuinely that Anna found herself pouring her heart out to him. A great listener, he never once interrupted her.

"We've been seeing a psychologist off-and-on for about two months now. Dr. Elliot says I have to give Nick more freedom. But how can I when I don't trust him? He lies to me and constantly disobeys me. Take last night, for example. He left the house when he was grounded, and then stayed out all night. I worry about how he's going to survive out in the world with a bunch of strangers when he can't even be civil to his own mother."[18]

Anna's hurt and resentment dissolved the moment she lifted her gaze and looked into the teenager's mesmerizing eyes. Nowhere on his countenance could she find a hint of judgment. He didn't accuse her of being a bad mother. He continued to smile at her, despite the awful truths she was bombarding him with. Relieved to have said everything in her heart, she lapsed into silence. The rustling of the woodland animals gathering food for the winter ahead broke the stillness.

Finally, the young man spoke. "You cannot build a loving relationship with your son until you learn to love yourself."

Anna stared at the boy. "What?"

The kindness in the youth's eyes never wavered, although his brow furrowed slightly. "I'm certain that your son loves you, and I can see that you love him very much. The question is, 'Do you love yourself?'"

Anna's mouth fell open. "But...I mean, how... Of course..." Her voice trailed off.

The boy shrugged. "When you look in the mirror, do you like what you see?"[19]

Before she could formulate a reasonable answer to his question, he leaned forward and touched one of her hands. "I have to go. Maybe we'll meet again. I like to walk in the woods when the weather is nice, and this is where I like to meditate." In one graceful movement, he stood up. "Follow me, and I'll show you the path."

Without looking back to see if she followed, he jumped down from the rock and crossed the stream on the back of a fallen tree. Anna scrambled to catch up with him.

Tall for his age and lean, the teenager strode ahead with the assurance of an experienced hiker. Anna had to jog to keep up with him. At the top of a steep incline, he looked around and smiled at her. "The entrance to the park is just ahead." As graceful as a deer, he veered off the path, slipping between the trees and branches, leaves crackling beneath his feet.

"Wait," she called back, unwilling to let him go so easily. "I don't know your name."

From a distance, she heard his reply carried by the wind. "My friends call me Hawk."

Anna walked home from the park, her feet on automatic pilot, her head in the clouds. She couldn't stop thinking about her encounter with Hawk. His question circulated through her mind repeatedly. "When you look in the mirror, do you like what you see?" No one had ever challenged her this way, especially a teenager who could be a friend of her son's.

Since Kevin's sudden death four years ago, Anna had been forced to focus most of her time and energy on survival. Mortgage payments on the house she and Kevin had bought because it sat in an excellent school district absorbed more than half her income, and she tightly budgeted the rest. The little free time she had left after wrestling with her finances went to working in her garden or bailing Nick out of whatever trouble he had gotten into. In all those years, she had never once taken time out of her hectic life to plumb the depth of her feelings about herself.

Still reeling from the effect of Hawk's words, Anna entered her house and took the stairs two at a time. She stripped off her exercise clothes and turned on the shower. Before she stepped into the welcoming steam, she turned to the medicine cabinet and stared into the mirror.

At age forty-three, she was still a pretty woman, although she had deep worry lines burnished into her forehead and dark bags under her eyes. She leaned closer and studied her face, trying to see more than her physical traits.

Mist from the shower clouded the glass, but not before she glimpsed the cold truth. She *didn't* love herself. Hell, she didn't even *like* the person who frowned back at her from the mirror.

Shivering, she stepped into the shower, letting the hot water sluice down her, washing away the dirt that lay on the surface of her body.

At work, Anna lost herself in the office maelstrom, catching up on yesterday's postponed jobs and tackling new crises as they arose. She called home twice, and when Nick didn't answer, she forced herself to put aside her anxiety and focus on her work. She had decided to take Carol's advice and leave Nick alone. She tried to believe, as her friend insisted, that he just needed some breathing space.

Instead of taking a lunch break, Anna munched on an apple and kept working. By five o'clock, she had cleared her desk of everything except the two new projects that had come in late in the day.

Filing the papers in her TO DO folder, she grabbed a damp sponge from the sink and wiped down her desk. She watered the plants that hung in her window and crowded her windowsill, then put on her navy blazer and reached into her file drawer for her purse. Before turning off the lights, she surveyed the neat, organized space and smiled. She had accomplished a great deal today, and she had hardly worried about Nick at all.

Anna's pleasure was short-lived. The closer she got to home, the more her anxiety level rose. What if Nick hadn't come home? What if he had forgotten they had an appointment with Dr. Elliot in forty-five minutes? How would she explain his absence to the psychologist without making herself look like a weak parent?

She parked the car in front of the house, relieved to see the front door standing partially open. Nick was home. Usually, she would get on his case for forgetting to shut the door, but she was so happy he was back that the small indiscretion seemed too trivial to mention.

"Nick?" she called. "You home?"

There was no answer, but she could hear the beeps of a video game in progress in the basement. She leaned into the stairwell and called again. "Hey, Nick. I'm home. You want something to eat before we go to Dr. Elliot's?"

He still didn't answer, so she went down the narrow steps. He was sitting on the floor, his back against a steel beam, intent on the action on the screen in front of him. His slender fingers flipped between a bewildering array of buttons and knobs on the controller.

"Come on, buddy. Finish your game. We have to leave for Dr. Elliot's in a few minutes."

Just then, the car he had been skillfully racing around a debris-strewn track crashed into a guardrail and exploded. Nick threw the controller down and turned on her.

"See what you did? That's the highest level I've ever gotten to in this game. I could have beat it if you hadn't made me lose my concentration."

He flipped a switch on the base and started a new game.

"Hold it right there, Nicholas. Turn that machine off. Now! We can't make Dr. Elliot wait so you can play a video game."

Without looking at her, Nick said, "I'm not going."

Anna's anger rose. "What do you mean, you're not going? After everything that happened at school yesterday and what's going on between the two of us, you have to go."

"I don't want to. I'm waiting for a phone call."

She tried cajoling him. "Come on, Nick. Can't you finish your game later?"

He took his eyes off the screen long enough to glare at her. "No!"

"Dammit, Nick—"

"You go. You're the one who needs a shrink."

"Nicholas!"

The phone rang. Ignoring his mother, Nick froze the action on the screen and picked up the portable waiting by his side.

"Hey, Kelly," he said, all the anger gone from his voice, a smile appearing like magic on his lips.

Expelling a long breath as loudly as she could, Anna spun around and stomped back up the stairs. Okay, so a conversation with his girlfriend was more important to Nick than settling things with his mother. She could handle that. And she *would* go to see Dr. Elliot by herself. Why shouldn't she? Her HMO's mental health coverage had expired last session, and she was stuck paying for this appointment out of pocket whether anyone showed up or not. She would have to work through the humiliation of arriving at the session without her son, but she might end up getting something out of seeing Dr. Elliot alone.

Anna arrived on time, and the middle-aged psychologist immediately ushered her into his office. She sat on the comfortable couch, and grabbed one of the colorful throw pillows, hugging it to her. For a few minutes her embarrassment kept her tongue-tied, and she couldn't meet the psychologist's gaze. Instead, she concentrated on pulling at a tuft on the little pillow.

Finally, Dr. Elliot said, "I assume Nick isn't coming."

She nodded. Encouraged by the kindness in his voice, not sensing any disapproval of her for her inability to coerce her teenager into cooperating, she looked up. He smiled at her.

Anna liked order. She usually brought Dr. Elliot up to date on Nick's behavior and their skirmishes in chronological order, incident by incident. Today, however, knowing that she had the whole hour to herself, she broke with her normal pattern. She didn't talk about the latest crisis at school or about Nick. Instead, she talked about herself.

"The strangest thing happened to me this morning. When I was out walking, I met a teenager named Hawk. He was sitting on a rock meditating, if you can believe it. He didn't look any older than Nick, but he sure didn't act like any adolescent I've ever met. Hawk was so quiet and—I don't know—I guess you'd have to say he seemed wise beyond his years. He listened to my latest beefs about Nick and didn't make me feel stupid or petty. I felt totally at ease with him, like he understood what I was going through even though he should have been more on Nick's side than mine." She stopped talking and looked at Dr. Elliot. "Have you ever run into anyone like that? Someone that is so much older than their physical years?"

The doctor nodded. "If you were Hindu and believed in reincar-nation, you'd call him an old soul—a human who has been reborn many times, achieving a higher level of consciousness on each of his journeys."

She leaned back and pondered what Dr. Elliot had said. "You know what he asked me when I had finished telling him about my dysfunctional relationship with Nick?"

The doctor shook his head.

"He asked me if, when I looked in the mirror, did I like what I saw."

"And?"

She laughed, trying to make light of the shocking revelation that had come to her as she stared into the bathroom mirror this morning. "Funny you should ask. I decided I don't like what I've become. Somewhere along the way, I got lost. I've been so busy trying to hold down a job and raise my son without any help that I haven't had time to be with myself. I don't think I know who I am anymore." She turned to the psychologist. "What happened? When did I lose track of my life?"

"When do you think you did?"

Anna sighed. "I guess the obvious answer is when Kevin died. But maybe it was before that."

"Most of us spend our entire lives trying to find ourselves or to figure out who we are." He paused, then added, "Perhaps by pondering this question, you will learn about yourself and also grow as a parent."

A surge of excitement passed through her. Now they were getting somewhere. "So, you think Hawk was on the right track?"

"His question was certainly thought provoking. I think you might learn something from him. As Nick's contemporary, his perspective on your relationship with your son could be invaluable."

Anna frowned. "Yeah, I guess so, although Hawk seemed so much more mature than Nick."

"I don't judge a person's spiritual development by his or her chronological age. I've seen teenagers who are much more in touch with their true selves than their parents are."

Anna laughed nervously. "I hope you're not implying that about Nick and me."

Although Dr. Elliot smiled reassuringly at her, Anna wondered if he hadn't really meant to show her, in a nice way, how backward she was as a parent.

"Why don't just the two of us meet for a few sessions and explore your feelings about yourself a little further? When you can look in the mirror and see the good person you know you can be, we'll stop."

"But what about Nick's therapy? I can't afford more than one session a week."

"The best thing you can do for him right now is to learn about yourself. Besides, he doesn't want to come, and I don't think we should force him to. We'll see where our work together takes us first."

Anna looked at her watch. She couldn't believe an hour had already flown by, and she hadn't said one word to Dr. Elliot about Nick's school suspension. And she wasn't going to. But the highly organized woman inside her wouldn't let her leave without something more tangible than a few slippery "truths" to bat around until their next session.

"Don't you have some reading material or an assignment that I could get started on before we meet again?"

Dr. Elliot thought for a moment. He scribbled something on the pad he kept on his lap. "Here. Try to do this by next week."

Anna glanced at the page. Scribbled across it was a single sentence. "Spend some time looking at yourself in the mirror and write down twenty words or phrases that describe what you see."

She carefully folded the sheet and placed it in a pocket of her handbag. "I'll do it. Thanks, Dr. Elliot."

"When you look at yourself in the mirror, try to stay away from physical descriptions, Anna. Go for character traits."

She frowned. "I'm not sure I understand what you mean by character traits."

"Well," the psychologist explained, "instead of saying 'I like my brown hair,' you might want to say something like 'I'm generous.'"

She nodded. "I get it." Pivoting, she left the doctor alone in his office, busily writing up his notes from their session.

Relief flooded through her. Her first solo meeting with Dr. Elliot had gone well. She was actually looking forward to finding out about herself. She got into her car and headed home with the intention of doing the exercise the moment she walked in the door.

Nick heard the car door slam. He stared out his bedroom window at the Saab, watching his mother gathering her things off the front seat and opening the car door. He debated how to handle her inevitable appearance in his room. Turning his boom box up to top volume was one way to keep her from nosing into his business. Or he could turn out the lights and pretend he was asleep.

Nick was a little worried about what his mother and Dr. Elliot had talked about. The psychologist had been pretty good about telling his mom to get off his back in the past, but now that he wasn't going to the sessions anymore, there was no one to tell the shrink the truth about what was happening around here. What if Dr. E. gave up on him? What if he and his mom decided to get tougher on him—like no TV, no video games, no leaving the house, stuff like that? He'd have to move out then, maybe go live with Bob. Since his parents were so cool, they might not mind him staying over there for a while.

Nick got up and turned off the stereo. He flicked off the lights and hopped into bed, pulling the covers over himself, fully dressed. He listened to his mother's footsteps on the stairs. To his surprise, she passed by his room and entered the bathroom that connected their two rooms instead. For a long time, he didn't hear anything, not even the water running. What was his mother doing in there?

His curiosity piqued, he got out of bed. Careful to make as little noise as possible, he tiptoed across the room to the bathroom door. Placing his ear against the wood panel, he heard what sounded like the whimper of a wounded animal. Kneeling, he peeked through the keyhole. His mother was leaning over the sink, staring at herself in the mirror. Tears streamed down her face as she tried to muffle her sobs in the sleeve of her sweater.

Nick's heart began to pound. He didn't want his mother to fall apart. Adults weren't supposed to lose it like that. Sure, he and his mom fought a lot, but she was the only parent he had. He got to his feet and hurried downstairs to the TV room. He'd watch a few shows and stay out of his mother's way. He'd give her the space to get herself together that she never allowed him.[20]

4

For the rest of the week of Nick's suspension, Anna didn't get a chance to return to the park to look for Hawk, whose glowing face and mesmerizing eyes popped into her mind at odd times. She worked day and night. She barely saw Nick, which was probably a blessing since the stress level at the Sullivan Agency reached an all-time high Wednesday night, then continued to climb as the crew revamped Upland Petroleum's advertising campaign. Somehow, the creative staff met their Friday deadline and went home for a well-deserved two-day rest. Even Gerry left on Friday a happy man. The only person who didn't get a break was Anna. As office manager, she was saddled with cleaning up the mess left by the frantic rush to complete the job and five days worth of other clients' work to catch up on.

After a hellish weekend working both at the office and at home, Anna awoke early Monday morning. Although tired and out of sorts, she would not go another day without exercise. She dressed quickly. Her sneakers laced tightly, an old sweater of Kevin's thrown over her exercise outfit to shield her from the October chill, she stepped gingerly out of the house and began her usual warm-up circuit of the neighborhood.

For a while, Anna's mind filled with to-do lists for work and home. However, the soothing cadence of her body in motion slowly relaxed her. She stopped worrying about the responsibilities that awaited her at the end of her walk and lost herself in the physical pleasure of walking.

In a trance-like state, she let her body dictate her course. Before long, she found herself in the park, clambering down the path she had discovered the week before. Her unconscious desire to speak with Hawk suddenly became palpable. She wanted to tell him what she'd seen in the mirror. A keen sense of anticipation taking hold of her, she threw caution to the wind and began to run, hopping across logs and sliding down leaf-strewn paths, somehow knowing she wouldn't make a misstep.

The sound of rushing water became more distinct. She slowed her pace and caught her breath, her heart beating wildly, and not from physical exertion. Here she was, the mother of a teenager, getting nervous about meeting one of his peers.

As she approached the turn in the path that, if taken, would expose her to Hawk's scrutiny, Anna suddenly felt shy and unsure of herself. She stepped into the bushes, craning her neck to see around the corner. The sight of Hawk sitting on the rock deep into his meditation sent a thrill of anticipation through her.

As if he could sense her presence, Hawk, his eyes still closed, called out to her. "Hi, Anna. Why don't you come across the stream and hang out with me for a while?"

Anna stared at the creek, swollen from a recent spate of rainy weather, and felt a sharp stab of disappointment. The rocks and log she had used to ford the stream last week were submerged in the rapidly moving current. She couldn't see any way to get across the water without ruining her expensive cross trainers, which she shouldn't have bought in the first place and couldn't afford to replace.

She emerged from the bushes and threw up her arms. "I can't get across. There's no way."

Hawk opened his warm brown eyes and smiled at her. "Of course there's a way. There's always a way."

"But the water's too deep. I can't do it. With my luck, I'll probably fall in and drown."

"If you try to see the possibilities, not the probabilities, you'll find a way to do it."[21]

Anna walked up and down, examining the streambed. She gauged the distance from bank to bank. Could she jump that far? Maybe at the narrowest point. She moved to her left a bit and backed up several paces. From this vantage point, the creek didn't look quite as formidable. She had run track in high school and was light on her feet. Maybe she could jump across. She played out the leap in her mind.

"When you're ready, jump," Hawk encouraged her, his voice soft and compelling, as if he were convinced she couldn't possibly fail.

Anna took a deep breath and backed up another yard. She counted to three and began her run. At full stride, her lead foot slammed down on a large rock by the water's edge. Pushing off, using her arms to give her added momentum, she flew into the air. She hung over the water, her whole body trembling with unbridled exhilaration and sheer terror. When her feet hit the dirt on the opposite bank, her forward thrust sent her sprawling on all fours, but she had done it. She had vaulted across the swollen stream.

Standing up, she brushed the dirt from her palms and knees. She accepted Hawk's offer of a hand up and found her spot on the rock. Even on this chilly day, the spot remained warm, as if he had prepared it in advance for her.

In her excitement, she blurted out, "I didn't think I could do it!"

Hawk, who had already returned to his cross-legged posture, looked at her with his kind eyes. "You must have thought you could do it. Otherwise, you wouldn't have made the leap."[22]

Anna wasn't quite sure what he meant, but she was too caught up in the exhilaration of the moment to concern herself with it.

A faint smile lingering on his lips, Hawk asked, "Would you like to learn how to meditate?"

"I don't have the patience for that sort of thing. I couldn't sit still and do nothing."

Hawk tilted his head, his eyes boring into her. "Is that what you think meditation is? Sitting still and doing nothing?"

Afraid that she might have offended him, she quickly added, "Oh, no. I mean, it's just not for me."

"Would you like more peace in your life?"

"Yes."

"Then meditation is for you. For centuries people have used meditation to tap into infinite wisdom and stay centered in the midst of chaos."

The tranquil smile on Hawk's face elicited one from Anna. "Okay, you've convinced me. I'll give it a try." Feeling a little foolish, but knowing that no one she knew would see her, she copied his posture, sitting Indian-style and placing her hands, palms up, on her knees. She let her eyes drift shut.

After a few minutes, Hawk's soothing voice drifted over to her like a dandelion seed in the wind. "Breathe with your mouth closed. Focus on the passage of air through your nostrils. Breathe in, breathe out. As random thoughts enter your mind, simply observe the beginning, middle, and end of the thought. Then gently but firmly refocus your attention back to the breath."

She concentrated on her breathing and quickly got the knack of relaxing into each breath. Thoughts and images from the previous week floated into her consciousness. She concentrated on prioritizing a list of things she needed to get done at home and at her job.

Anna worked at her list for a few minutes, but had trouble letting go of her thoughts to allow new ones in. Getting antsy and no longer able to concentrate, she opened her eyes and saw Hawk watching her.

"What happened, Anna?"

"I was doing okay, but then I had trouble letting go of my thoughts and refocusing on my breath. I think I just have too many things going on in my life right now."

He smiled at her, his eyes glowing. "I challenge you to make time for meditation every day. I promise it won't take long to see results. You may even find that you have more time for other things once you start meditating regularly."[23]

His prediction didn't make sense to Anna, but she thought she might try this meditation business. If it was what made Hawk so wise beyond his years, then it was worth pursuing. She could use a little wisdom right about now. Especially after her revelations while looking in the mirror.

As if he could read her thoughts, Hawk asked, "When you looked in the mirror, Anna, did you like what you saw?"

"How did you know—" She cut herself off, realizing how ridiculous her question was. Of course Hawk knew she had looked in the mirror. She wouldn't have come to see him again if she hadn't.

She took her time formulating her answer. "No. I didn't like what I saw. My eyes didn't shine like yours do, and there were dark rings under them. I was frowning. The woman in the mirror was a lonely, unhappy person who didn't like anything about her life." Anna's voice caught. She had to force herself to say aloud her next observation. "And, worst of all, I saw that she was a terrible mother."

Unable to look into Hawk's eyes any longer, Anna dropped her gaze to the pendant he wore around his neck. For the first time, she noticed the image of a dragon etched into the luminous green stone. The piece was unusual, and she wondered where he had gotten it. When she screwed up the courage to glance back up at his face, she was rewarded with a kind smile. He didn't seem the least bit perturbed that she had confessed her inadequacies as a parent to him.

The loud cawing of a bird put an end to their silent reverie. Hawk slowly unwound his limbs and stood up.

"I have to go, Anna. You don't need me to guide you out of the park today."

She nodded. "You're right. I can find my way."

She stood and dusted off the back of her sweatpants. With a pang, she realized she didn't want her time with her young friend to end. "When will I see you again? Will you be here tomorrow?" she asked hesitantly.

His long, dark hair blowing in the wind, the lanky teenager nodded. "If you need me, you'll find me."

Anna's heart expanded with gladness. She wanted Hawk to be here for her every day. She wanted to pour out her sadness and grief to him because, somehow, she knew this mysterious youth could spin her sorrows into gold.

She jumped down off the rock and mentally prepared herself to cross back over the stream. She assured herself that she could do it. That she had done it before. That anything was possible. Although an adrenaline rush made her heart pump faster and her limbs tremble, she raced down the bank and leapt into the air.

She landed hard on the opposite embankment, safe and dry.

Hawk's voice drifted over to her. "When you look in the mirror, can you see Nick?"

It took her a few seconds to regain her breath. "What?" she asked, not certain she had heard Hawk correctly. Twisting at the waist to look back across the stream, she searched the shadows, but he was gone.

She walked briskly along the path toward home for a few minutes before a sudden realization hit her, making her stop dead in her tracks. Hawk knew her name. He had known it from the first day they met—but she had never introduced herself to him. Had she?

She shook her head as if to clear it. Hawk's uncannily accurate readings of her needs, his quiet acceptance of her faults, and his strange questions confused her. She usually ran away from anyone who challenged her the way he did. But her intuition told her that she had met Hawk for a reason, that listening to him and answering his questions were key to her becoming a better person and a better parent to her son.

Once she was out of the woods, she put her thoughts about Hawk behind her and picked up her speed. It was almost seven. She hoped Nick had set his alarm clock and gotten himself up for school. On his first day back, it wouldn't do to get a detention for tardiness. He had to prove to his teachers that he was serious about toeing the line, or the rest of his years at Shady Hill High would be tainted.

Anna bounded up the steps and into the house. She shut the door, listening carefully. Silence greeted her. She didn't hear running water, or the teakettle whistling, or the dryer door slamming—sounds that indicated Nick was awake.

The mellowness and feeling of power she had experienced after leaving Hawk disappeared in a cloud of anger. For God's sake! The boy was fifteen. Why couldn't he get himself out of bed? Now he was going to miss his bus, and she would have to take him to school.

Anna stormed up the stairs, banging hard on her son's bedroom door. "Nick! Wake up! Do you have any idea how late it is? You already missed your bus."

She waited, but heard nothing. She banged again, her voice rising. "You better get your lazy butt out of bed right now, or I won't be able to take you to school. Get up, Nicholas."

She heard a crash. He'd tripped over the phone wire and sent the extension flying again. She'd already had to buy a new telephone after the last time he carelessly dropped it.

The latch on his door clicked, and Nick, his eyes barely cracked open, his hair sticking out in all directions, emerged. He headed for the stairs and bumped into her. Instead of apologizing, he shoved her out of the way.

Incensed, Anna followed him down the steps, her voice shrill, even to her own ears. "Is that the thanks I get for saving your ass? If I hadn't been here, you'd still be asleep. With your grades and your reputation as a troublemaker, you can't afford to miss any more school."

He entered the half bath under the stairs, slammed the door in her face, and locked it. "Aren't you going to take a shower?" she demanded.

His silence infuriated her. She stormed back upstairs to the bathroom they shared. Just because her son chose to be a slob didn't mean that she had to be one.

She turned on the shower and waited for the hot water pummeling her skin to sooth her. Today, however, the cleansing ritual did little to calm her, and she was still angry as she toweled herself off.

Leaning over the sink, she glanced at herself in the mirror. Her face was red, especially high on her cheekbones, and her hair was a mess—just like Nick's. The eyes shining back at her were filled with deep-seated resentment and roiling anger. It was a look, she suddenly realized, she often saw in her adolescent son's eyes.

Hawk's words echoed in her head. "When you look in the mirror, can you see Nick?"

When she grasped the meaning implicit in the question, Anna's mouth fell open. Hawk had wanted her to see the similarities between Nick and herself. Blinded by his physical resemblance to his father, she had always scoffed when people claimed her son took after her. Now she saw that they did look alike—however, it was not his bone structure that resembled hers, but his facial expressions, which mimicked hers perfectly.

A chill raced down Anna's spine. What kind of legacy was she passing on to her son? Trapped in a stressful job she hated, worried constantly about money and keeping up the house, she had become a bitter, lonely adult. By her example, was she condemning Nick to a similar fate? Could it be that the very behaviors and attitudes that she detested in Nick were her own, passed down from one generation to the next? That she became so easily annoyed at her son because he mirrored her own personality flaws? Did Nick's behaviors trigger so much anger in her because she was angry and disappointed in herself, not her son?

She tore her eyes from the mirror and let her head fall into her open palms. She was supposed to be the adult in this relationship, but she had been acting like a child.

Anna shook her head to clear it. Something had to change around here, and she was beginning to realize that she was that something. She looked at the clock and swore under her breath. It was seven-twenty already, and she wasn't dressed. She quickly threw on some clean clothes. Placing the wealth of papers she had sorted through over the weekend in a large cardboard box, she rushed downstairs. She really didn't have time to make breakfast, but it had been ages since she and Nick had eaten together.

A wave of indecision rolled over her. They would both be late if she made French toast and bacon, but she ought to spend some time with her son trying to mend the rifts that were tearing them apart.

Making up her mind that the world wouldn't end if she and Nick were late this morning, she threw an apron over her outfit and got to work. When Nick stumbled into the kitchen ten minutes later, she had the table set with place mats and napkins, juice glasses, and a plate stacked high with French toast and fresh-cooked bacon.

His shocked expression made the effort worthwhile. No doubt, he had expected her to nag him about his irresponsible behavior, not make food for him.

"Would you like to join me for breakfast, hon?" she asked tentatively.

At first, she thought he might refuse. His eyes scanned her face for any hint that she had ulterior motives for her kindnesses. Apparently satisfied that she had no hidden agenda, he dumped his book bag on the floor and slid into his chair.

Anna knew better than to push their fragile peace. She contented herself with watching him wolf down his food and drink two glasses of juice. Another day, after she figured out this whole parenting thing, she'd try to engage him in a meaningful conversation. For now, being in the same room with Nick and not fighting felt really, really good.[24]

Surprisingly, Anna's good mood held up under the strain of returning to the office. There was a sense of excitement in the air, a feeling that the staff had worked as a team on an impossible job, and they had emerged victorious. Even Gerry was feeling magnanimous and complimented Anna on the neatness of the office. Despite her resentment at having to work through the weekend, the praise made her feel warm inside.

When the phone rang right before lunch, she answered it in a light, pleasant tone.

The second she recognized the voice on the other end of the line, her heart sank. She hadn't expected to hear from Ms. Blackmun on Nick's first day back at school, especially after the nice morning they had shared. "What's wrong?"

"I don't think you should be too upset by this, but Nick got into a disagreement with his Spanish teacher again. He came into class a few minutes late, and Mrs. Johnson gave him an after school detention. Nick didn't take to the punishment very well. After he let his teacher have it verbally, he left the classroom and came directly to see me."

"What did you do?"

"Nick gave me the distinct impression that he didn't want any more trouble. It seems that he presses Mrs. Johnson's buttons and visa versa. I'm trying to rearrange his schedule so I can transfer him into another section."

Anna's ire began to rise. These young counselors gave in too easily. "Don't you think it would be better for Nick to stick it out and learn to put up with someone he doesn't like? What message are you sending him? That when the going gets tough, drop out?"

"I'm sorry that you think I'm not being tough enough, but I feel Nick needs some extra nurturing right now. I'm going to do what I can to get him out of that Spanish class. Have a nice day, Mrs. Farmer."[25]

Anna placed the phone in its cradle. She fussed with the piles of paper on her desk, feeling powerless to make a decision about what to attack first.

"I'm on my way to the deli for lunch. Want to come?" Carol stood in the doorway, a worried expression on her face.

"What's your problem?" Anna snapped.

"You! You're my problem! Everyone else is on Cloud Nine around here, thrilled with the creative work that went into the Upland job, and you look like the Grinch just stole your Christmas."

Anna pushed her hair off her face. "Sorry. I'm tired, that's all. I had to work all weekend, and there are still a zillion piles to go through." She swept her hand around her desk to indicate the chaos she faced. "I can't take time for lunch."

"Everyone needs a break, kiddo. Get your jacket, and let's go."

Anna realized she wouldn't get anything accomplished in her present state, so she relented and followed her friend out of the building. When they had settled into a quiet booth at the rear of the busy deli, Carol asked her, "What's wrong, honey? It isn't just work, is it? Is Nicky giving you a hard time again?"

Anna was always amazed at how well her friend could read her mind, although it wasn't hard to guess what was bothering her these days. She was always upset about Nick.

"Yeah. We had a fight because he didn't get up in time to make his bus, but we made up and actually had a civil breakfast together. I was in a good mood until his school counselor called to tell me that he'd gotten into a verbal confrontation with one of his teachers." She looked into her friend's sympathetic eyes. "I don't know, Carol. If he gets any more difficult, I won't be able to handle him at all. He's bigger than I am and doesn't listen to a word I say."

"How's his therapy with Dr. Elliot going?"

"It's not. Nick refuses to go, so I'm taking his place."

"Great! I think that's a terrific idea." Carol smiled broadly.

Anna laughed nervously. "Is it that obvious that I need help?"

"We all need support, Anna, and you haven't had any since Kevin died. I go to see Roberta, my former therapist, when I feel I need a tune up. Seeing a shrink is nothing to be ashamed of."

At that moment, the waiter arrived and the two friends ordered their lunches. As soon as he disappeared into the kitchen, Anna asked, "Why in the world would you, of all people, see a therapist? I've never met a more together person, even if you sometimes are a little flaky."

Carol laughed, pushing her gray bangs out of her eyes. "Babe, what you don't know about me would fill a book. I've worked hard to get where I am today, and I'm proud of it. Things haven't always run this smoothly in my life, you know."

"Poor Carol. She stubbed her toe once, and it was black-and-blue for a whole week!"

Carol ignored Anna's attempt at keeping the discussion light. "Is that what you think? Do you really believe Frank and I had it easy raising twin girls? In your wildest dreams you can't imagine what their early adolescence was like!"

Anna waved a hand dismissively. "Come on, Carol. Your girls are great. You have the perfect family. Don't tell me Tracey or Ellen ever got suspended from school, or verbally attacked their teachers, or hung out with the blue-haired crowd."

"You met me after we had weathered the worst of the adolescent storm. Trust me, Anna. Those two tested us. When Tracey was fourteen, we discovered she had been experimenting with drugs and was drinking heavily. She even ran away for a few days. Then, when the twins turned fifteen, Ellen became clinically depressed, and we had to hospitalize her for three weeks."

Anna was so surprised by her friend's revelations that she remained speechless. She noted the pride that shone in Carol's eyes.

"Those girls were a handful, but we all got through the bad times. And look how well they turned out."

At that moment, their sandwiches arrived. Anna was glad of the interruption, which gave her a chance to digest Carol's revelations.

After swallowing a few bites of food, she asked her friend, "If you could pinpoint the one thing that turned your kids around, what would it be?"

"That's a tough question. So many factors were involved, including the natural process of growing up. But if you pushed me, I'd have to say the greatest gift I gave my kids was the work I did on myself."

"What? You mean you didn't have to set up contracts, make rules about curfews, or send them to counseling or anything like that? The girls just changed because you did?"

"Oh, we did all that stuff, but I truly believe it was my work on me that turned things around. Once I got a sense of myself and learned to like myself, I handled the kids a lot better. Having peace of mind helped me see the big picture, and I didn't worry so much about life's annoying details. I stopped losing it every time one of the girls did something irresponsible or stupid, and I was able to curb my screaming matches with the little beasties. Unless we were all PMSing at the same time, our lives ran a lot more smoothly after I got my priorities straight."

Anna hadn't touched her food since Carol began speaking. It was impossible to imagine that her gentle, goofy friend had ever been out of control with her kids. She always spoke so highly of them, and when they visited her at the office or took her out to lunch, the three of them laughed, bantered, and carried on like the best of friends.

Carol reached across the table and took Anna's hand. "I know you think that Nick's behaviors are what are causing you to lose it with him, but it doesn't have to be that way. You're the adult. It's within your power to step away from the drama. Trust me, Anna. Get your own life in order, and you and Nick will get along much better."

A weight lifted off Anna's shoulders. Hope welled up inside her. Maybe someday she would share with Nick the kind of relationship Carol had with her girls. Anything felt possible. Even that someday she, Anna Farmer, might become a wise, compassionate friend to a younger woman the way Carol had been to her.[26]

When they finished their meal, her friend left the cash on the table, with Anna covering the tip. They headed back to the office arm in arm. Anna smiled. For the second time in one day, her spirits soared. She resolved to do her best to keep her temper under control and not let Nick's behaviors get to her.

Before she went to bed that night, Anna placed a big overstuffed pillow on the floor and sat in the center of it. Feeling ridiculous, she nonetheless crossed her legs, placed her hands, palms-up, on her knees, and closed her eyes. She had no expectations other than to give the weird Eastern tradition Hawk had introduced her to another chance. She focused on her breath and tried to remember what the youth had said about observing the rise and fall of her thoughts and feelings.

Images of the day just past came racing into her consciousness. She saw Nick's tentative smile, flashed at her over their shared breakfast. She saw Carol's kind face beaming at her across the lunch table, giving her hope and courage. Then her own face appeared, staring back at her from a mirror. For the first time in a long while, she liked what she saw. Her eyes were smiling.

As suddenly as the visions of her first good day in weeks flashed through her mind, they were gone. She became aware of the creaking of the house around her. The pipes banging in the basement announced the drop in temperature, which meant heating season and an increase in her energy costs had begun.

Grumbling at herself for being so gullible as to think that sitting around on a pillow could solve her problems, Anna pulled down the covers and got into bed. Immediately, she fell into a deep slumber.

5

Anna dreamt about Kevin. She saw him in the supermarket, bent over the frozen foods. When she called his name, he turned and held out his hands to her.

Rushing into his arms, she cuddled against his warmth. "I've missed you so much."

He kissed the top of her head. "I'm sorry, Annamarie. I'm sorry I left you alone."

"I'm okay, Kev."

He hugged her tightly to his chest. "I know you are. You'll be fine."

Anna pulled away from his embrace to search her husband's face. "It's Nick I'm worried about. He's so hostile to me these days. And he's hanging out with a bad crowd."

Smoothing his hand across her cheek, Kevin smiled at her. "Have faith in our son, sweetheart. He loves you very much. He's scared, that's all."

The warm glow that surrounded them began to fade. Anna reached out to grab for Kevin, but he was gone. She opened her eyes, and found the spare pillow clutched to her chest.

In the past, her dreams of Kevin had been nightmares, swirling with angry despair and unrequited needs. This morning, Kevin's loss seemed almost bearable. Perhaps the worst was behind her. Perhaps the wounds of grief had begun to heal.

She dressed quickly for her morning walk, eager to find Hawk and tell him everything that had happened yesterday. It was hard to believe that it had only been twenty-four hours since they had last met in the park and he had taught her how to meditate.

She didn't bother to make her circuit of the housing development, but headed directly for the park. She scrambled down the first steep hill, catching a glimpse of a lanky figure moving gracefully through the undergrowth not far ahead. She knew immediately who it was.

"Hawk!"

He stopped and turned, waiting for her to catch up. "Hi, Anna," he said in his quiet voice, his eyes smiling a greeting. "Want to walk together for a while?"

"Yeah. That would be great." She adjusted her stride so she could keep up with him. "A lot's happened since I saw you yesterday. I got really pissed with Nick when he didn't get up in time to make the bus yesterday morning, but I made up my mind that I wasn't going to be the evil ogre. I made him breakfast and we actually had a nice time. I didn't even mind that I was a few minutes late to work because I had to take him to school."

"Why?"

Anna looked up over at Hawk, puzzled. "Why what?"

"Why did you get angry with Nick when he didn't get up in time?"

"Because he missed the bus, and I knew I'd have to take him to school."

"Why?"

"Why what?"

"Why did you have to take him to school?

"Because I'm a single mother. Who else was there to do it?"

They walked on in silence for a while. Anna thought they had exhausted the topic until Hawk asked, "Whose responsibility is it to go to school?"

She looked up at him, but he kept his gaze directed on the path ahead. "Nick's?" she responded tentatively.

"So?"

"So what?"

"So, why did you have to take him to school if school is his responsibility?"

Trying to keep her growing exasperation out of her voice, Anna answered evenly, "Because Nick is irresponsible. If I didn't take him to school, he wouldn't go. He's been in enough trouble already this past week. He doesn't need to add truancy to his record."

"Maybe he does."

Anna had had about enough of Hawk's weird responses. She stopped walking and stood in the middle of the trail with her hands on her hips.

Hawk's strides shortened, and then he stopped and turned to face her.

"Are you trying to tell me it would be in my son's best interest to skip school? That's a joke, right? You're just saying that because you're a kid yourself." Even to her ears, the words rang false. Hawk wasn't just another kid. Ashamed of her outburst, Anna was relieved to see that Hawk wasn't upset.

He took a step toward her, his eyes still gentle and smiling. "Nick won't take responsibility for his own life until you let him. You have to let him make mistakes and pay for them, Anna."

"But—"

"He'll never get up by himself if you keep bailing him out. Can you see that?"

Damn this upstart kid. What he said sounded crazy, but it made a weird kind of sense.[27]

Hawk laughed. "Come on. I'll race you to the creek."

Forgetting that she had stopped running several years ago after a knee injury, Anna gave chase. Because the teenager's legs were much longer than hers, the race was no contest, but she wasn't far behind.

They arrived at the brook to find the water level up again. Hawk didn't slow his pace, jumping the stream as if he were merely striding over a log. With the confidence of an Olympic long jumper, Anna adjusted her stride and followed. To her astonishment, she hit the ground a full foot in front of where Hawk had landed.

She dusted her hands off and stood up. He had already climbed the rock and assumed his meditation pose. She joined him, his words still ringing in her ears. *Nick won't take responsibility for himself until you let him.* She had always assumed that the way to get Nick to grow up was to point his faults out to him. Nagging him, as he would say, to do the right thing had become a way of life. Maybe she was being too conscientious.

Positioning herself on what she now considered to be her spot on the rock, Anna watched Hawk cross his legs and close his eyes, undecided as to whether she should join him. Her rational mind told her that meditating was stupid and a waste of time, but she had felt a surge of power after trying to meditate last night, and then she had experienced the wonderful dream about Kevin. Maybe—

No! She could see how some people who weren't as rational as she was could benefit from sitting on their asses and doing nothing, but she had too much to orchestrate in her complicated life to waste her time on something that might or might not help her.

She fidgeted, trying to keep from exploding while Hawk finished his meditation. During her wait, she studied the intriguing pendant he always wore around his neck. The dragon carved into the green stone appeared to stare directly at her. A beam of light from the rising sun sent a slice of sunshine across the youth's chest. The medallion shimmered.

Anna looked up and saw Hawk's warm eyes focused on her face. To cover her embarrassment at being caught staring at his chest, she asked, "Does your necklace have a story behind it? It's very unusual."

Hawk fingered the pendant with one hand. "A shaman gave this to me. It's made of malachite, a stone the ancients believed had transforming powers and could ward off evil. The dragon symbolizes strength and wisdom." He reached up and took it from around his neck. "Would you like to hold it?"

Anna nodded. Hawk placed the talisman in her open palm. Where the stone touched her, her skin tingled, as if the energy of countless generations radiated through the amulet to her. She ran the tips of her fingers over the carving, amazed at the detail etched into so small an area.

Shaking her head in amazement, she returned it to him.

"You are afraid to meditate." His statement threw her off, coming as it did out of nowhere.

"It's not that I'm afraid of meditating, it's just not for me. I can't slow my mind down so that thoughts can drift in and out of consciousness. Hell, I don't even know what consciousness really is."

"You want to try something that could make everything clearer, Anna?"

"Sure, I guess. What?"

"Look in my eyes."

She stared into pools of iridescent amber.

"Where are you, Anna?"

Mesmerized by the glow of his eyes, she found herself assuming the same position as Hawk, legs crossed, hands on knees. "I'm in the woods sitting on a rock."

"Where are you, Anna?"

"In the woods, with you."

"I mean, where are you in your head?"

Anna tried to keep the exasperation out of her voice. "I'm wondering why you're asking me where I am."

"Where are you, Anna?"

"I'm thinking this whole conversation is really weird, and I'm trying to figure out what you think you're accomplishing by asking me the same question over and over again."

"Where are you?"

"I'm thinking that it's getting late and I need to go to work soon."

"Where are you, Anna?"

"I'm right here!" she blurted out.

Hawk's face broke into a grin. "You got it."

Anna looked at him, wondering which one of them was going crazy. "Got what?"

Hawk stood, swung himself off the rock, and headed into the woods.

"Got what?" she called after him.

He stopped and looked at her for a moment. "Mindfulness."

"What's mindfulness?"

"Being in the here and now."

"What does mindfulness have to do with meditation? I don't get it."

Hawk smiled at her. "You will." Without a sound, he disappeared into the forest.

Anna reached over and touched the spot where the boy always sat. His warmth lingered. She looked up through the tangle of branches and thinning leaves. The sun had burned off the cloud cover, taking some of the chill out of the air.

Standing, she stared toward the spot where he had disappeared. Hugging herself, she whispered, "Where am I?" then answered herself. "I'm here. I'm in the here and now."

Anna retraced her steps, leaving the park behind but unable to solve the riddle the inscrutable teenager had posed. Approaching her home, her practiced eye automatically scanned her front flowerbeds. She still had to dig up the annuals before the first real frost, then add mulch to prepare the beds for winter. Maybe she'd splurge and order some Dutch tulip bulbs. That would give her something new to watch for in the spring. Liking the sound of the idea, she made a mental note to call Carol and have her bring in one of her gardening catalogues. Anna would put in an order today before she had a chance to change her mind.

Entering the house, she stood in the entranceway and listened. The upstairs was ominously quiet. No creaking floorboards or clanging pipes. Nick had obviously slept through his alarm again. Yesterday she had knocked loudly on his door and complained bitterly about his irresponsible behavior. Today, she wouldn't play the same old game. No more Nagging Mother Syndrome. She would stay out of Nick's business and see what happened.[28]

After showering and dressing for work, she ate her breakfast, stuffed her papers in her briefcase, and left a note for Nick on the kitchen table. She had completed her responsibilities as a mother. It was up to Nick now.

Instead of the guilt she had expected, Anna felt proud of herself. She made it all the way to the Sullivan Agency without picking up the cell phone and calling her son.

At the office, she went about her morning duties in a daze, waiting for her telephone to ring, rehearsing what she would say to Nick when he called. When she couldn't stand the wait any longer, she went looking for Carol, finding her at her drafting table. Anna explained what she had done.

"Good for you, sweetheart. I'll bet Dr. Elliot will be proud of you."

Anna loved Carol, but she didn't think her friend would understand that it wasn't a professional who had urged her to let Nick suffer the consequences of his irresponsible behavior, but a boy her son's own age.

"I suppose so, but I don't know what to say when Nick calls and accuses me of not caring about him."

"How about, 'I'm not a rooster or an alarm clock. You need to get yourself up and to school in the morning.'"

"He'll scream bloody murder."

"Tell him you love him and hang up."

"What if he doesn't go to school?"

"Then he'll have to pay the piper. It's not your problem anymore, Anna. The kid is almost sixteen."

"Okay, okay, I get it. I need to stop taking on things that are my son's responsibility so my son can be more responsible, right?"

"Exactly."

Anna decided to ask Carol if she had ever heard of mindfulness. To her surprise, her friend nodded.

"Sure. Mindfulness means being in the moment."

"Great. That's a big help."

Carol laughed. "Okay, let's say the phone rings right now and Nicky says the very thing that will set you off. How about 'You are the worst mother in the world.' Would that do it?"

Anna grinned. "You bet."

"Okay, so your automatic reaction to his statement would probably be to strike back, yell at him, right?"

Anna hung her head. "Unfortunately, yes."

Carol glanced up from the drawing board, an earnest look on her face. "That's because you've already decided in your head that a 'good' mother wouldn't let her son get away with that kind of bratty behavior, right? You'd be remembering all the other nasty things Nick has said to you in the past and, maybe, if you were like me, you'd be projecting this battle of the wills well into the future. How am I doing so far?

"You're right on, sister."

"What if you didn't let yourself get all worked up about the past or didn't predict a future that may not happen, but just cleared your mind and stayed in the moment? No judgments about Nick or your parenting skills or what he just said or did. Can you see how you might handle the situation differently if that were the case?"

Anna tried to imagine mindfulness the way Carol described it. "Basically, I'd have to space out, not pull out my sword of righteousness and attack, the way I usually do." She frowned. "I don't know if I can make my mind turn off like that. But if I could, I would probably feel a lot less stress and be a whole lot happier."

"You got it, babe. You're a quick study. It took me a whole weekend at my yoga retreat to figure that one out."

Bolstered by Carol's confidence in her but still nervous about her reaction to Nick's expected blow up, she returned to her office. She jumped every time her telephone rang. Finally, she picked up and it was her son.

His voice heavy with sleep, he said, "Mom, it's ten-thirty."

Anna glanced at her watch. "That's right."

"Why didn't you wake me up?"

"What happened to your alarm clock?"

"I forgot to set it."

"Oh, well, I'm sorry you overslept."

"Ma. How am I gonna get to school? Besides, I can't go without a note explaining I was sick this morning. I'll get a detention. You have to come home."

This was the hard part. Anna wanted desperately to bail Nick out. Just this once. If she did, maybe he'd understand how much she loved him.

She took a deep breath and carefully considered her words. "Here's what I'm willing to do. I'll come home, pick you up, and drop you off at the high school, but I won't write a note telling a lie. And next time you're late, you'll have to walk."

"*FORGET IT!* I won't go to fucking school."

The line went dead.

"Damn!" Anna muttered under her breath. "I can't win with that kid." She started to slam the receiver down, but stopped herself. She gently replaced it in its cradle. She had to break the pattern. Letting her anger take over would only get in the way of resolving her problems with Nick.

Taking several deep breaths and closing her eyes, she forced herself to relax. She focused on her breathing. "Where am I? I'm right here," she told herself and found to her surprise that her acute anger pangs became more bearable. Reopening her eyes, she found Carol leaning against her door, her arms folded across her chest, a smile on her lips.

"I guess Nick called."

Anna nodded. "I offered to give him a ride to school, but I told him I wouldn't write him an excuse for being late. He went ballistic and hung up on me. I tried to relax and stay out of my head. I think it worked a little."

"You're doing fine, Anna. Don't worry. He'll come around. Just hang in there."

"God, this getting tough stuff is so hard!" Anna exclaimed.

The friends shared a laugh, then Carol gave Anna some artwork to copy and fax to a potential new client.

After her friend left, the phone rang again.

"Hello, Mom?"

"Yes, Nick?"

"I'll take that ride to school now."

Anna dropped what she was doing. "I'll be home in ten minutes. Be watching for me."

Anna breezed through the rest of her day. For the first time in many months, her response to Nick's anger had not been a return volley. She had relaxed and the situation hadn't gotten out of hand. She could have been tougher on the kid and not gone home to get him, but she had held firm about the note. He knew she meant business, and he wouldn't forget to set his alarm again soon. At least she hoped he wouldn't.

Arriving home to an empty house, Anna was relieved to find a message from Nick on the answering machine. He was staying after school for detention and would be taking the late bus home.

While the message played, conflicting emotions warred inside her. She was proud that her son sounded so grown up and had acted so responsibly, but she was sad, too. In a real and deeply painful way, she was losing him. He was growing and changing right before her eyes. It wouldn't be long before he graduated high school and left her forever.[29]

Shaking off her sense of doom, she grabbed a quick bite out of the refrigerator. She had to rush because tonight marked her second appointment with Dr. Elliot, and no one or no thing would stop her from getting to his office on time. She left a ten-dollar bill on the kitchen table with a note telling Nick to order out for dinner.

Twenty minutes later, Dr. Elliot ushered her into his office and sat in his regular chair. Anna took a seat on the couch. She handed him a slip of paper. "Here's the list of twenty personality traits that I saw in the mirror last Tuesday night. I cried like a baby when I realized how low an opinion I have of myself."

Dr. Elliot took a few moments to read the list to himself. Then he read a few aloud: "Angry, stressed out, unsupported, lonely, bad mother. How do you feel about these now that a week has gone by? Has anything changed for you since you identified these traits?"

"Yeah, a lot has changed. I had two more encounters with the teenager in the park. He tried to teach me about meditation and mindfulness. And he asked me another question: 'When you look in the mirror, can you see Nick?'"

"And?"

"And the answer is 'Yes.' I see the same angry, sour expression on his face that's usually on mine. I see that he's as unhappy as I am."

"Is there anything you can do about that?"

Anna hesitated. Her eyes darted from Dr. Elliot's face to her folded hands. "I can keep coming here and working on myself so I'm not such a lousy role model for my son."[30]

"Good. Did anything else happen this week?"

"My friend Carol has two wonderful daughters who are in their twenties. When I asked her how she produced such great kids, she said the greatest gift she gave her daughters was the work she did on herself."

"She's right. Learning parenting skills is important when you're dealing with a volatile teenager like Nick, but using new techniques without changing your attitudes won't improve your relationship that much."

"Yeah. I think I'm beginning to get it. If I learn to control my anger and start acting in an appropriately adult manner, Nick won't have anyone to fight with. Automatically, our lives will be better."

Dr. Elliot took off his glasses and polished them with a handkerchief he drew from his hip pocket. "I wouldn't say 'automatically,' but it will definitely be another step in the right direction."

She glowed with the praise. "I didn't wake Nick up this morning. When he called me at the office and was really angry with me, I didn't let his temper tantrum get to me. Everything worked out fine, and afterwards, he treated me with more respect than he has since he was little."[31]

The loss implied in her words hit Anna like a runaway truck slamming into a cement barrier. She missed Nick the way he used to be. She missed the happy boy who had respected her authority and made her appreciate the importance of her mission as a mother.

She started crying. At first, she tried to hide her tears from the psychologist, but when he offered her a box of tissues, she began to sob. When she finally got herself back under control, she wiped her eyes and gave Dr. Elliot a weak smile.

"You miss the little boy Nick used to be," he said.

His kind words perched her on the precipice of another bout of crying. She didn't dare speak, so she nodded.

"What you're feeling is totally normal, Anna. What parents of teenagers have a hard time realizing is that everything—and I mean *everything*—changes when a child hits puberty. In infancy, a child is totally dependent on you, the benevolent being who tends to his every need. A first-time parent knows all about the awesome sense of responsibility that comes with the arrival of a baby.

"In childhood, the parent still takes on a lot of responsibility. He or she is charged with keeping a child safe and growing in a healthy manner. The adult still makes the majority of important decisions in a child's life.

"Adolescence is a time when the roles begin to shift. Teens become more responsible for what goes on in their lives. Parents find this transition extremely difficult.[32] In your case, I'd say it's been more traumatic than most because of the stress of losing Kevin so suddenly."

A part of Anna wanted to jump up and scream, "Yes! None of this is my fault. I'm a victim of circumstance." Another part acknowledged that she had accepted the role of victim without a fight, directing her anger over life's capriciousness at Nick.[33]

"I know. I'm supposed to allow Nick to make his own decisions. But he's so irresponsible. It's hard to watch him botch things up."

"The process is called independence, Anna. Nick is headed there whether you want him to or not. The question is, can you let him go?"

"There are those words again. *Letting go*. Everyone keeps telling me I have to, but I don't want to."

"What's the most important role you've played in your life?"

She stared at Dr. Elliot. "Being a mother, I guess."

"And Nick's march toward independence threatens that role, right?"

"If you put it that way, yes."

"Then having a teenager in the house threatens who you've been for the past fifteen years, the person you identify with. Nick's change is challenging *you* to change. Letting go of the old you and defining a new you—particularly in terms of your relationship to Nick—is scary. The transition is scary for Nick, as well. There's a part of him that doesn't want the relationship to change."[34]

Anna shook her head. "I don't see that at all. He's always yelling at me to get out of his life, to leave him the hell alone."

"But he wants you to wake him up and take him to school, doesn't he?"

"That's just because he's lazy. Besides that, when I do, he ignores me."

A slow smile crossed Dr. Elliot's face. "Adolescence is a tough, confusing time in a child's life. I think Nick is as scared as you are by all the emotional upheaval going on inside him. He still needs to know you're there for him."

Now confusion clouded Anna's dawning awareness. "But I thought I wasn't supposed to wake him up, that he'll only learn to be independent by making mistakes."

"That's correct. I didn't say that I thought that you should wake him up."

"Then what am I supposed to do to let him know that I love him?"

Dr. Elliot shifted in his seat. "Tell him."

"I do. All the time. He either gives me a funny look or ignores me."

"That's pretty typical teen behavior. Nick has to show you how tough he is, but he still wants you to tell him you love him." The psychologist paused. His intense gaze fell on Anna, making her squirm in her seat. "There *are* other ways to show him how you feel that are more subtle, and, I believe, more powerful."

"Like what?"

"Like listening to him rather than arguing with him, or keeping that negative comment about the clothes he's wearing to school to yourself. Things like that."[35]

"I'll give it a try."

"Good."

Their time was up, so Anna made an appointment for the following week and left Dr. Elliot's office. On the drive home, she turned on the radio and sang along to the soft rock songs on her favorite station. By the time she arrived home, she had the volume cranked up and was singing in her rusty soprano with total abandon.

Nick heard his mother's car pull into the driveway. Turning off the video game he had been playing, he went upstairs to meet her. He needed a ride to Bob's house to pick up a new CD his friend had bought for him at the mall.

From the top of the basement stairs, he caught the strains of music. Curious, he went to the center hall and peered out the window. His mouth dropped open at the sight that greeted him. His mother lounged in the car singing along to an old Cat Stevens' tune he recognized from his childhood. When the song ended and he saw her gathering up her things, he raced back to the kitchen. He didn't want his mother to know he had seen her.

He timed his approach so that he was just emerging from the kitchen when the front door flew open. His mother rushed in, a huge smile on her face. She caught sight of him, and her grin broadened. "Hey, Nick. How are you?"

He stuck his hands in his pockets and stared at the floor. "Good. Listen, can you give me a ride to Bob's? I need to pick up something of mine he has."

Nick's shoulders scrunched in a defensive posture, but the angry words he expected didn't materialize. His mother's hand alighted on his shoulder. He looked up slowly. She was still smiling. Even her eyes were smiling. "I need to grab a bite to eat, then I can take you. Fifteen minutes okay?"

He didn't want to smile, but he couldn't stop himself. His mother actually looked happy, and that made him happy. "Yeah, that's cool. Thanks."

He started to pull away, but she gripped his shoulder more firmly. "Nick, have I told you today that I love you?"

His eyes flitted up to meet hers, then dropped. He swallowed hard. He couldn't speak.

Undaunted by his silence, she continued. "I just wanted you to know that I'm sorry for some of the shitty things I've said to you recently. I really am glad you're my son."

Spring

6

Anna didn't need her alarm clock to wake her now that the birds had made their vocal return from the south. Their joyous songs pierced the early morning air. Anxious to get outside and walk, she sprang from bed, dressed quickly in her exercise gear, and bounded down the stairs and out the front door. She stopped on the final porch step to take in a lungful of the loamy odor that arose from her garden. The tulips she had planted last fall had broken the soil's surface, but hadn't yet bloomed. Her crocus and snowdrop blossoms had come and gone, leaving only the early daffodils as harbingers of her garden's future glory.

Satisfied with what she saw and anticipating time over the upcoming weekend to get down and dirty in the garden, she sighed contentedly and set off on her walk. During the unusually cold and snowy winter that had just passed, Anna had been forced to curtail her walks, avoiding the park altogether because of the dangerous conditions on the hilly trails.

Today, with the sun shining and the smell of spring in the air, she would try the park. She hoped that Hawk would be out now that the weather had changed. The few times she had made it to his rock

83

during the winter, he hadn't been there. She had missed seeing him and talking to him. Now that she had been practicing meditation and mindfulness for a number of months, she had become a firm believer in the power of the process.

She and Dr. Elliot had made great progress, too, and she wanted to show off the new woman who had emerged out of the darkness. After five months of therapy, Annamarie Farmer liked herself, and she wanted the world to know. She had learned to stand up to her obnoxious boss, on more than one occasion leaving work early when the stress got to be too much for her. Her son was treating her with more respect now that she had learned to use mindfulness to defuse her temper and didn't always go off on him when he pushed her buttons.

She was still worried about Nick's erratic behaviors, especially since he was turning sixteen in a few weeks and had started putting pressure on her to let him get a driver's license. She doubted seriously that it would happen any time soon. She had told him he needed to maintain a "B" average to drive, and his grades hadn't been that high since middle school.

She took her time descending the steep part of the path, holding onto branches to keep from sliding in the mud. After the trail leveled off and the conditions improved underfoot, her pace quickened. Before long, she could hear the creek bubbling over the chirping of the birds and the pounding of her own feet.

She turned the last bend, her eyes eagerly seeking a familiar form and was relieved to see Hawk. A slight breeze moving wisps of hair around his face, he sat on the outcropping in his meditation position— legs crossed, palms up and resting on his knees.

Although she was quite certain she had made no noise, she could tell by the smile that spread across his face that he felt her presence. "Anna. Welcome back."

She shook her head, amazed as always by the youth's powers of perception.

The spring runoff from the mountains made the stream look more like a river. Instead of panicking at the sight, Anna took her time to assess the situation. Although too wide to jump, the rapidly flowing water had uprooted a tree along the bank. Anna climbed its branches and crossed over to the meditation rock without incident.

She settled into her spot, crossing her legs in a half-lotus position like a professional yoga. Meditating had become so much a part of her life that she didn't have to remind herself to concentrate on her breath, but experienced deep relaxation almost immediately.

Completing her meditation, she opened her eyes. Hawk pinned her with a gaze that sparkled with compassion. "Do you love yourself yet, Anna Farmer?"

Anna flushed. "Yes. I think so. At least I'm much happier than I used to be."

His eyes never left hers. "When you look in the mirror, do you love and accept yourself totally and without judgment?"

She hadn't expected Hawk to challenge her this way. Not so soon. Uneasy, she let out a braying laugh. "I'd have to take a look at that one. I mean, I'm getting better, but I'm still not perfect."

"Can you love and accept your imperfect self totally and without judgment?"[36]

She wrinkled her nose and threw up her hands in mock resignation. "Are we getting into something important here? Should I be taking notes?"

Hawk smiled at her. "Until you can truly love yourself as you are, how will you be able to love and accept Nick as he is?"

Anna broke off eye contact. She folded her arms around her knees, staring at the budding trees over Hawk's shoulder. "I don't know what you mean. Nick's doing much better now that I've gotten off his case. What else do I need to do?"

"What is your biggest problem with Nick now, Anna?"

She didn't hesitate. "School work. Grades. He's such a smart kid, but he's lazy. If he tried, he could do much better."

"What makes you think he's not trying? Maybe he's doing the best he can under the circumstances."

Anna snorted. "What circumstances? The kid's got it made in the shade. He doesn't have a job. He spends all his free time going to the mall or the arcade with his girlfriend and his buddies. That's why he isn't doing well in school. He's too busy having fun."[37]

"One of his most important jobs as a teenager is to explore relationships and make a space for himself in the adult world. Is Nick doing that?"

"I suppose."

"Then he's working hard. He's doing the best he can, just the way you are."

Anna didn't know how to respond. Everything Hawk said went against what she had been brought up to believe. Her parents had stressed that schoolwork and commitment to family came first. Spending time with friends and developing relationships hadn't even made it onto the top ten list of appropriate activities for a teenager.

"I disagree. Nick isn't doing the best he can. There is no excuse for his grades. He knows he has to do better if he's going to get any scholarship money for college."[38] She screwed up her courage and let her eyes drift back to Hawk's face. He didn't look angry, or even concerned that she had contradicted him. His eyes continued to smile at her without any sign of disapproval.

"It's not easy letting go of our judgments. You've tried and convicted Nick of laziness and purposeful disrespect of your wants and desires for him. Have you ever sat down and asked him what he wants and desires for himself? Have you ever told him that, no matter how badly he screws up, you love him?"

A pang of remorse stabbed at her heart. Despite the progress she had made on herself, she was often at odds with Nick over his irresponsible behaviors. She only pointed out his failures to him to make him understand how everything he did now would affect his future. "I tell him all the time that I love him," she said, going on the defensive, "but I can't condone his irresponsibility."

There was that smile again. Hawk was obviously enjoying their sparring match. "When Nick does badly in school, do you hug him and tell him you love him anyway?"[39]

Anna laughed. "Yeah, right. If I did that, he'd think his mother had been kidnapped and an android had taken her place."

Hawk stood up, offering Anna a hand. They faced each other, energy vibrating between them. "Try it. Maybe you'll be surprised." With his usual abruptness, he jumped off the outcropping and disappeared into the woods.

Anna took a few moments to reacquaint herself with the sounds of the forest, which she had completely blocked out during her conversation with Hawk. When the rushing water, the rustling branches, and the whistling birds had worked their magic and she felt ready to return home, she hopped off the rock and scrambled over the fallen tree to the path.

Nick jumped in the back seat of Squeak's old Ford Galaxy. Of course, she had more kids crammed into the car than there were seatbelts, but no one cared. It was the first decent spring day, and the lunch crowd was hyped. Driving on the expressway to get to Taco Bell for lunch, windows wide open and the wind whipping his hair in his face, Nick could almost forget his worries. Kelly hadn't called him in a week, and she had been too busy "studying" over the weekend to go out with him. He had a bad feeling about where their relationship was headed—into the dumpster unless he did something about it.

And he dreaded the scene that awaited him at home. Report cards had gone out yesterday. His was sure to be in today's mail. Unfortunately, he had promised Allison that he would stay after school to help her with her senior science project. If he didn't get home before his mother and hide the damned report card, all hell would break loose. He'd be grounded forever.[40]

Nick had thought his school troubles were over when he'd sweet-talked Ms. Blackmun into moving him out of Mrs. Johnson's Spanish class. Although he liked Signora Martinez a lot better, he still didn't get

Spanish. His teacher had taken him aside this morning and told him he had failed the marking period. She had suggested he find a tutor and work hard for the remaining quarter, or he'd have to repeat Spanish next year.

At the fast food restaurant, Nick couldn't eat. He sat on the periphery of the crowd and pretended to listen to the high energy conversation swirling around him. No one noticed his moodiness, and that was okay with him. The kids he went to lunch with were upperclassmen. He was lucky they accepted him. The last thing he needed was to have them find out how messed up he was.

The rest of the school day was torture. Although he knew he couldn't race right home after last period, he still watched the clock relentlessly. When the final bell rang, he considered bugging out on Allison—saying he forgot or something—but his sense of honor wouldn't let him. He owed the senior class president a lot. If not for her friendship, he wouldn't have been accepted by the older kids and would still be sitting in the cafeteria with the other fifteen-year-olds at lunch, waiting for one of his classmates to get a driver's license.

He met Allison in the psychology department office.

"Hey, Nick. Thanks a lot for coming. I need to test a ton of kids to get enough data to prove my hypothesis."

"What are you trying to prove?" he asked, curious despite his eagerness to be done with the project.

"I can't tell you until after you take my test. Now, get comfortable. You can take your shoes off, if you want. I'm setting up a few things in the other room. I'll only be a few minutes. Don't come in until I tell you to, okay?"

Nick nodded. He waited in the office, at first amusing himself with reading the different posters that lined the walls. When he had read every one at least twice and Allison still hadn't returned, he sat in a chair, trying to get comfortable by slouching. He had grown about six inches since the summer, and his lanky frame barely fit the chair. There was no way to relax in it.

Within minutes, he was up again. He checked himself out in the large mirror on the wall. Satisfied that there were no new outbreaks of pimples on his face, he scraped at the stubble on his chin with his fingertips. He had just started shaving and found the new growth encouraging, a sign of his new status as a man.

Glancing at his watch, he realized that twenty minutes had already gone by, and Allison still hadn't come back. Now he was getting pissed. He was doing her a favor, a big favor. He'd probably get in trouble with his mother because of this favor. The least Allison could do was stick her head in here and tell him why things were taking so long.

He stared at the door. She had told him not to come in, but she had also told him she'd only be a few minutes. Allison hadn't kept her side of the bargain. Why should he?

He moved to the door. He was reaching for the handle when a thought occurred to him. This was all part of the experiment. Allison was waiting to see what he'd do. She might even have the door rigged so he'd get an electric shock if he touched it. This was a psychology experiment, after all.

He stared at the mirror, which suddenly looked more like a window than a mirror. Two-way, he bet, like what the cops used to interrogate prisoners.

Now certain that he "got" what Allison's experiment was all about, he racked his brains for the most outrageous thing he could do. Taking off his clothes and dancing on the desk naked was pretty extreme, but there was no way he had the guts to do it. However, he could pretend to go ape shit and scare the crap out of her. That would work. He had plenty of experience throwing tantrums. All he had to do was pretend his mother had locked him in here to punish him for his bad grades.

Before he gave himself away by laughing, he started pacing the room, mumbling under his breath. "It's not my fault, don't you understand? I suck at languages. I can't learn Spanish. It's too hard. I don't understand it."

His muttering became louder. "I'm not trying to hurt you. I'm doing my best. Can't you understand that?"

He wasn't acting any longer. The words flew from him in a tirade. "Let me the fuck out of here. You can't do this to me. It's against the law. I have rights, too, you know. I'm a human being."

A hand encircled his forearm. He spun around. Allison, her face white, stared up at him. "Nick? Are you okay?"

He hadn't even heard her enter the room. For a few seconds, the hopelessness that had overwhelmed him still kept him hooked into his anger. Finally, he shook it off and said, "Yeah, I'm fine. Did I win an Oscar for that performance, or what?"

He tried to smile confidently at Allison, but his lips trembled. He swiped the back of his hand across his mouth. "I figured out what you were up to and thought I'd give you some memorable data for your experiment."

Allison sighed and released his arm. "God, Nick, you had me scared for a minute. How did you make yourself so angry?"

He shrugged. "It was easy. I imagined my mother screaming at me when she opens my report card tonight and finds out I flunked Spanish."

"Oh, Nick. I'm so sorry."

"That's okay. I can always take Spanish in summer school or repeat it if I don't pass the year."

"I can tutor you if you want. I love languages. However, that's not what I meant. I meant that I'm sorry that you and your mother don't get along. I'd hate it if my mom yelled at me because I got a bad grade."

Nick shrugged. "You mean there are parents who don't scream at their kids for fucking up?" He tried to laugh, but the strangled sound that came out of his mouth sounded more like a bomb going off. He spent ten minutes filling out a form describing how he had felt in the isolated room, and then Allison took him home.

As she drove down his street, Nick craned his neck to see ahead. His heart jumped when he saw the Saab already parked by the front door. "Shit. She beat me home."

Allison stopped at the bottom of the drive. "Don't let anyone tell you you're not great, Nick, because you are. The senior class president of Shady Hill High School says so." She leaned over and gave him a kiss on the cheek. "See ya. And thanks for staying after school to be my guinea pig. You were by far the most original subject I've tested so far."

"You're welcome, Madame President." He hauled his book bag out of the car and trudged up the short hill toward home.

He entered the house as quietly as he could. Dropping his bag by the door, he checked the pile of mail on the radiator. His report card wasn't there. Either he'd gotten lucky and the letter was lost in the mail, or his mother had it and was waiting to pounce.

"Nick, is that you?"

Her voice came from the kitchen. Nick scrambled up the stairs. He'd reached the first floor landing when his mother appeared below him, dressed to go out.

"I have an appointment with Dr. Elliot. I'll be home in an hour or so. I made macaroni and cheese and a salad. You can eat now if you're hungry, or wait for me to get back."

"Okay, Mom." Nick scurried to his room, shutting the door behind him. What had just happened? Had his mother opened his report card or not? She hadn't seen Dr. Elliot in almost a month. Why was she running off to an appointment now?

On the drive to Dr. Elliot's office, Anna gave herself a mental pat on the back. Although she had wanted to wait in ambush for Nick and confront him with the glaring "F" on his report card the instant he walked in the door, she had heeded Hawk's advice. Instead of losing her cool, she had called Dr. Elliot. Luckily, he had just had a cancellation and could see her. She would run the whole issue of grades and responsibility past him and see what he suggested. Surely he wouldn't agree with Hawk that Nick was doing the best job he could? Dr. E. would talk about consequences and making Nick more responsible, but he wasn't a teenager like Hawk. He'd support her views of what had to be done to put an end to Nick's shoddy school performance.

Once in his office, however, she learned how wrong her supposition was.

"Nothing? You're saying I should do nothing to punish Nick for failing Spanish?" There had to be a conspiracy against her. Nick and Hawk had somehow brainwashed Dr. Elliot. "How can I let my son get away with this? You're the one who's always telling me that kids need consequences. What's the consequence in this case?"

Dr. Elliot gazed at her for a moment before answering. "There's something called a natural consequence, Anna. In this case, Nick will suffer several."

"Like what?"

"Well, he could very well fail Spanish for the year. It's humiliating for a teenager to have to admit to his peers that he's repeating. Next year he'll be competing with younger kids, and they might do better than he does. Then there's the issue you're so worried about. His record for college. Don't you think it bothers him that he's screwing up his chances for a scholarship?"

Anna scoffed. "Nick doesn't care. I'm not sure he even wants to go to college."

"Have you asked him what he wants? Does he think of himself as college material?"

"He should. I keep telling him how smart he is."

"What happened the last time he brought home a bad grade on a report card? Do you remember?"

Her face reddened. How could she forget? She'd totally lost it. "I got mad and called him a stupid idiot. No, a stupid *lazy* idiot. Not one of my better moments."

"How do you think that made Nick feel?"

"Pissed off and embarrassed."

"How did you feel?"

"Guilty and angry. Really stressed out."

"What would be a better approach? How could you turn this current problem into a win-win situation?"

Anna had to think. What was one of the most important lessons she had learned over the last several months of therapy? She had it! "I should not go off on him. I should step back from the drama."

"That's a good start, but there's more. Before you confront Nick, ask yourself the question, 'What's my goal here?' Certainly it's not to humiliate your son and send your blood pressure through the roof."

"No."

"What is your goal as a loving mother?"

"To get Nick back on track."

"Will humiliating him help him do better in school?"

"No."

"What if you simply told him that you loved him and would be there for him if he needed your help? How would that make him feel?"

"It would put the responsibility for change on him, and he would feel that I supported him."

"Exactly."

"But what if he keeps screwing up? Am I supposed to sit around and pretend it's all right with me that he's ruining his life?"

"Do you love your son, Anna?"

"Of course I do."

"Unconditionally?"

"With all my heart."

"Then don't judge him. He's living his life the way he needs to live it. Your job as his teacher is almost finished. Now you have to teach by example. Don't let him upset you. He'll find his own way."

"This is all part of that 'letting go' stuff I can't stand, isn't it?"

"The more you stay out of Nick's business, the happier both of you will be and the better your relationship will be."[41]

From behind the closed door, Anna heard a chair scrape on the floor. The psychologist's next patient had arrived.

"Nothing about raising kids is easy, is it?" Dr. Elliot asked as he rose from his chair.

"That's the understatement of the century. Do you have any parting words of advice before I return to the lion's den?"

"Remind yourself of your goal—to support Nick, not bash him. One way to beat teens at their own game is to do the unexpected. If

Nick expects you to lose it, don't. You'll throw him off, and he won't have anything to react against."

"That's an idea. I'm going to go home and try it."

Anna's heart rate climbed the closer she came to home. In a moment of weakness, she prayed Nick had already eaten and gone over to a friend's house so she could put off talking to him about his report card. She had to remember to think positively. Stay in the moment. Suspend all judgments. Let go of expectations. She knew all the buzz words. Now she had to live them.

She pulled the car in the driveway and turned it off. Nick's shadow appeared on the closed shade in his bedroom window. She saw him lift the corner to peer down at her. He knew she was coming, and he was probably scared to death to face her wrath. She had work to do.

Throwing her keys on the covered radiator by the door, she hung her coat in the mudroom and checked the macaroni on the stovetop. Nick hadn't eaten. She set the burner on low and tossed the salad. When everything was ready, she called upstairs. "Come on down, Nick. I've got dinner warmed up for us."

They had a pleasant meal together. From the relief on his face, Anna suspected that Nick assumed she hadn't seen his report card. He was about to clear the dishes when she said, "You did really well in English this marking period, son."

Gripping his plate with both hands, Nick stared at his mother. She wasn't yelling at him nearly as much as she used to before she started seeing Dr. Elliot, but still, she was his mom. She hated it when he did badly in school, and on this report card he'd brought home a big fat 'F' for the first time. She had to be pissed. Was she playing a game with him, waiting to hit him with the firestorm when he was relaxed, or was she really trying to make him feel good about his one and only 'A'?

"I like Mr. Daniels a lot. He used to play minor league baseball, and he pitched for Penn State."

"I'm glad you have a teacher you respect. How's the new Spanish teacher?"

Here it comes, he thought. "Signora Martinez? She's nice, but I still don't get how to study for her tests." He paused. When no explosion came, he added, "She told me I should get a tutor, or else I'd have to repeat the year."

"That's a good idea. Do you have anyone in mind?"

Nick brightened. Talking with his mother about his report card was turning out okay. "Yeah. Allison said she'd tutor me. You know how smart she is."

"Great. I'm sure you'll do fine with a little extra help. I had trouble with languages, too, when I was your age."[42]

"You did?"

"Uh-huh."

For the next fifteen minutes, Nick grilled his mother about her experiences in high school. He learned a lot about her he hadn't known. For example, her father had insisted that she work after school and had collected the money from her for her college fund. When she was ready to apply to schools, she found out there was no fund. Her father had spent all the money she'd earned gambling, certain that he would hit the jackpot one day. He never did. Now Nick understood a little better why his mother always harped on the importance of saving money and getting a college education. She had worked hard for the opportunity, and her father had taken it away from her.

They cleared the table and did the dishes together. Afterwards, before Nick headed upstairs, he said, "I'm going to call Allison right now and set up a study schedule."

"That's great, honey. Is there any way I can help?"

"No, everything's cool, Mom." He turned to leave but hesitated. "Thanks for being so understanding. I'm going to do a lot better next quarter."

His mother smiled at him. "I know you will, Nick."

7

"Yes!" Nick had thanked her for being understanding. Anna couldn't remember the last time he had complimented her on her parenting. Maybe things really had turned around. Maybe all the work she was doing on herself was making a difference with Nick, just the way Carol, Hawk, and Dr. Elliot had said it would.

Anna went upstairs to her room and closed the door. She pulled a pillow off her bed and sat on it to do her meditation. Hawk's question, "Do you love yourself totally and without judgment?" drifted through her mind. Right now, in this moment, she *did* love herself. And tonight she had proved that she could love her son, too, by letting go of her need to control his life. The rest was up to him.[43]

Nick woke up before his alarm went off. He felt great. He and Allison had set up a study schedule. He'd be meeting with her two days a week after school, and the night before every test she had agreed to spend extra time quizzing him on vocab and grammar. He smiled when he thought about the surprised smile he'd see on his mother's and Ms. Blackmun's faces when he aced Spanish this marking period.

At school, Nick didn't stop at his locker, but rushed upstairs to find Kelly before homeroom. Although spending so much time together was one of the reasons he'd done badly in school this year, he couldn't stay away from her. Being with her was like an addiction.

He navigated the crowded halls with the grace of an ice skater, taking the corner before her locker at a run and sliding into the space behind her with a big grin on his face. "Hey, Kel."

The moment she turned to face him, Nick suspected something was up. Instead of her usual cheery smile, she was frowning. "Nick. You scared me."

"Oh, sorry." For the first time, he noticed a guy standing next to Kelly. He recognized him immediately. Brian Esposito, captain of the hockey team. A senior. What was he doing here? Senior lockers were in the new wing.

"Nick, do you know Brian?"

"Yeah, sure. You were a pitcher at CAA, right?"

Brian stared at Nick as if he were a pest that needed extermination. "When I was twelve. So?"

Nick stared at Brian's hand, which rested comfortably around Kelly's waist. What was going on?

His gaze shifted to Kelly. Her throat and cheeks were splashed with pink. For a second their eyes met, then she looked down and whispered, "Sorry, Nick. I was waiting for the right time to tell you."

She might have said something else to him, but Nick had already zoned out. What an idiot he'd been not to realize Kelly had been giving him the brush-off for the last week. How could he possibly compete with a super jock senior? As far as Kelly was concerned, he was yesterday's bad news.

He turned abruptly and made his way downstairs, his feet getting him to the right place despite the fact that his mind was completely blown. Kelly had dumped him. He was alone again. Life sucked.

For the rest of the day, Nick went through the motions of going to classes, but he didn't learn a thing. He heard nothing his teachers or fellow students said. By dismissal, he felt like the walking dead.

"Yo, Nick!"

He turned to see Bob heading his way. Damn. The last thing he wanted to do was admit his humiliation to a friend, especially since, over the winter months, he had pretty much ditched his crowd for Kelly.

Bob looked as outrageous as ever. His hair was dyed red, white, and blue, and he wore it in an Afro. "Hey, man. What's up?"

Nick high-fived him, then replied, "Nothin' much."

"So, why don't you come to a party with us tonight? Zach Brommer's folks are out of town, and there's going to be a kegger. What do you say?"

Bob to the rescue. A party to get his mind off Kelly was exactly what Nick needed. Maybe he'd meet someone nice who'd make him hurt a little less.

"Okay. Sounds cool."

"You can spend the night at my house. That way you don't have to sneak out of yours. I know your mom can be a real bitch."[44]

Guilt shot through Nick. Although he didn't want to screw things up with his mom, he really needed to party with friends and mend his broken heart. He hesitated a moment, then took the plunge. "Sure, okay. I'll tell Mom that I'm sleeping at your house." He thought about putting in a few good words for his mother, who really wasn't such a bitch anymore, but decided to let Bob's comment slide.

Anna put the finishing touches on the supper she had made for herself and Nick. Despite the protestations of her demanding boss, she'd left work early to pick up ingredients for an Italian meal, exactly like the one Nick had made for her and she'd blown off last fall. She hoped he'd appreciate the symbolism of her menu choices. It felt as though the two of them had made an about-face since that terrible day in October, and she wanted to celebrate the changes.

Anna glanced at her watch and frowned. It was six o'clock, and Nick wasn't home yet. Even if he had stayed to study with Allison, he would have been home by now. She poured herself a glass of wine and waited. At six-fifteen, the telephone rang.

She picked up, relieved to hear Nick's voice. "Hi, Mom. I ran into Bob after school, and he invited me to spend the night at his house. We're going to chill and watch a couple of movies. Is that okay?"

Keeping her disappointment from her voice, she replied, "Sure."

"Great. I'll see you tomorrow, then."

"Nick!"

"Yeah, Mom?"

She had planned to ask him when he would be home in the morning, but stopped herself. Taking a deep breath, she said instead, "Have fun."

Anna returned the telephone to its cradle, briefly eyeing the kitchen and the set table. The irony of the situation wasn't lost on her. She had disappointed Nick and ruined his surprise last October, and now he had disappointed her.

Sitting back in her chair, twirling the stem of the wine glass between her fingers, Anna took a moment to think. She had two choices: sit around and feel sorry for herself, or get on the horn and find a friend to share the nice dinner she had prepared.

Nodding her head firmly, she drained the wine in her glass, put the glass in the sink, and picked up the phone.

This was more like it, Nick thought, settling into the back seat of Bob's car. His father, who managed a garage, had given Bob a vintage '72 Buick convertible for his sixteenth birthday. Although it was still too cold for any rational person to be driving around with the top down, that's exactly what they were doing.

Bob cruised the side of town Nick barely knew, picking up several of the guys, who climbed in back with him, and two girls, who sat together in the front bucket seat, giggling non-stop.

The frigid wind tore through Nick's hair, making him feel wild and free. Someone produced a six-pack, and after chugging a beer, he felt even better. Powerful. Today had been a nightmare but tonight would be all sweet dreams for him.

They arrived at the party a little before ten. Two burly seniors stood at the door of the house collecting money. Nick's self-assurance completely disappeared. What if Brian had brought Kelly to the party? Then everything would be ruined. He would have to spend the night sitting in Bob's car freezing his ass off.

The party was already in full swing, the noise deafening. Someone had thrown an old Led Zeppelin CD on the stereo in the living room, which was competing with The Roots' latest rap album blasting from upstairs. There were kids milling around everywhere.

Nick picked his way through the crowd, searching for Kelly and her new boyfriend. He'd made the complete circuit of the first floor and was about to head upstairs when a hand grabbed his upper arm and twirled him around. "Freddie? Where you been? I been lookin' fer you!"

A dark-haired girl about four or five inches shorter than Nick stared blearily up at him, a scowl on her face. "Shouldn't ditch a girl…" She hiccuped loudly, then laughed. "'Specially when she's had too much to drink."

To Nick's total amazement, the girl reached over and placed her plastic cup on the banister, grabbed both his hands, and pressed his palms into her breasts. "Come on! Come on, Freddie. Feel me. Feel how much I want you." She puffed her chest out, and he felt her nipples harden. Embarrassed, Nick quickly pulled his hands away.

A voice in his ear drew his attention away from the girl. "What kind of fool are you, anyway, Nick? The lady is dying to hook up with you. If you don't do it, I will."

Nick half-turned and was hit with a blast of Bob's beer breath. "She thinks I'm someone else," he whispered.

Bob laughed. "So much the better, my friend. No complications come morning."

The girl on the stairs was growing impatient. "Come on, Freddie. Les go back to the bedroom. You won't be sorry, big boy. Thas a promise."

The girl's hand slid suggestively down the front of his shirt heading toward a part of his anatomy that didn't need any stimulation. Nick grasped the girl's roving hand in his, shrugged his shoulders at his friend, and smiled sheepishly as she pulled him behind her up the steps.

The first room they found was occupied by another couple, as was the second, which turned out to be the source of the pounding rap beat. They finally found some privacy in a small room furnished with a twin bed and dresser at the end of the corridor.

The girl sat on the bed and flipped her sandals off. She patted the mattress next to her. "Cmmere, sexy," she said, grabbing Nick's hand and pulling him down next to her. They tumbled backwards, and before he knew what was happening, she was lying across his body. He closed his eyes, trying to imagine that the strange, wild creature in his arms was Kelly. Any pretensions he had were quickly dispelled when she found his lips. This girl didn't kiss at all like Kelly. Where Kelly was soft and pliant, this girl was hard and demanding.

Nick wondered whether he would be able to keep going with a complete stranger. This whole thing didn't feel right. His partner was drunk. She thought he was someone else. He really didn't like anything about her—except that she was available and more than willing.

He imagined what Bob and the guys would say if he backed down now. He'd end up with no girlfriend and no respect from his buddies. They'd laugh at him and call him a wuss.

He made out for a while with the girl, who rubbed her body suggestively against his, making odd, cooing sounds. God, what she was doing to him felt good. Real good. He forgot his earlier reservations and just went with the pleasurable sensations that rippled through his body.

The girl suddenly broke off their kiss. Nick opened his eyes and watched her sit up, kneeling on the bed with her legs straddling his body. She crossed her arms and caught up the hem of her mini-dress. With a broad sweep of her arms, she yanked it over her head, exposing soft breasts that practically spilled out of her sexy lace bra. Her only other item of clothing was a pair of matching thong panties. Nick stared at her lush body with growing excitement.

Obviously pleased with the effect her striptease had on him, the girl lifted a forefinger and flipped the bra's front clasp open, letting the wisp of material fall off her shoulders. Staring at her full breasts, feeling too hot to think straight, Nick helped her wriggle out of her panties.

The girl reached down, pulled his T-shirt out of his pants, and yanked it over his head. She popped the top button on his jeans and was working his pants down his legs when he finally came to his senses. What they were doing was wrong, and if he didn't stop this right now, he would end up regretting it. No matter how good he felt physically, he knew the difference between right and wrong, and this scene was definitely wrong.

Gently pushing her hands away, he tugged his jeans up and zipped them. She reached for his crotch, but he caught her by the wrists and held her away from him. He saw her large eyes fill with tears. "Hey, I'm sorry, but you're drunk, and we don't even know each other. This isn't right." He slithered out from under her and stood up. She collapsed onto the bed.

Nick heard the wail of sirens over the loud music coming from the room next door. He strode to the window and pushed the curtain aside. Two police cruisers, their lights flashing red and blue, pulled into the driveway. The incessant rap beat, which had been rocking the house, suddenly fell silent, replaced by screams and the pounding of feet.

"The cops," he said to the girl, who had curled up in the middle of the bed and was sobbing quietly. She didn't seem to hear him or sense the commotion taking place around them.

"Come on. Get dressed," he urged, eyeing the door nervously. "Didn't you hear what I said? The cops are busting the party."

The girl looked at him, her lower lip trembling, her mascara running down her cheeks along with her tears. "You don't like me, do you?

You think I'm stupid and ugly." Her face puckered and she began to cry again.

"Oh, Jeez. Come on. Don't do this. Please, stop crying and get dressed!" Nick's gaze swung wildly around the room as he looked for his shirt. He caught sight of a corner of it sticking out from under the girl's rear. As he leaned over to retrieve it, the door burst open.

"Hold it right there, buddy."

Nick twisted around, and the beam of a powerful flashlight hit him square in the face, blinding him. He put his hand up to protect his eyes.

The girl let out a piercing shriek. "He tried to rape me!" she shouted, grabbing the comforter to cover her nakedness.

Nick turned to stare at her. "What? What did you just say?" he asked, at first unable to comprehend the depth of her deceit.

A muscled arm came out of nowhere and grabbed him around the waist, yanking him off the bed. Someone pulled his hands behind his back. Nick heard the double click of handcuffs locking into place and felt the cold metal digging into his wrists.

Finally, everything came together. This girl, who he had never met before and whose name he didn't know, had told a lie to save her own skin, and he was in a shit load of trouble.

Anna had finished her meditation and was in bed watching the eleven o'clock news when the phone rang. This late at night, with Nick out, the ringing sent a chill down her spine. She slowly reached over to pick up the receiver.

Minutes after hanging up with the police, she was on the telephone with Dr. Elliot's answering service. "I need to speak to the doctor right away. My son's been arrested, and I don't know what to do."

"I'm sorry. Dr. Elliot is out of town at a conference. Dr. Friedrich is taking her emergency calls. Do you want me to page her?" a disinterested male voice asked.

Disappointment and fear flooded her mind and for a moment, Anna panicked. She quickly realized there was no point in waiting for a psychologist she had never met to call her back. "No, never mind. I'll take care of this myself." She dropped the phone and got herself dressed.

Heading downtown, her mind swirling in and out of reality, Anna drove on automatic pilot, not even aware of making turns or stopping for traffic lights. At one point, when the horrible truth hit her—that her son had been arrested for attempted rape—she had to stop alongside the road to cry, her emotions too overwhelming for her to handle.

She arrived at the impressive, pillared two-story structure in the center of town twenty minutes after receiving the call. She followed a police cruiser into the municipal lot behind the station. The sight of a stern officer exiting the car, his gun riding conspicuously on his hip, sent another wave of apprehension shooting through her. How could this be happening, especially now that Nick had calmed down and was taking more responsibility for his actions? Hadn't they just had an incredibly civilized discussion about his grades? Hadn't he worked out that sticky problem by himself?

Was her son capable of doing such a horrible thing? How could he be doing this to her?[45]

Shaking so badly she could barely pronounce her name to the duty officer at the front desk, Anna sat on a bench in the vestibule and waited. When the heavy bulletproof glass door swung open in front of her, she jumped up. A female officer in plain clothes, whose solemn expression and tough body language did nothing to allay Anna's fears, led her into the station house.

"I'm Officer Morris, Mrs. Farmer. If you don't mind, I'd like to talk to you privately before you see your son."

Anna had no idea if she should talk to the officer or not. Her only knowledge of legal matters came from the few courtroom dramas she had watched on television. She wondered if she should ask to see an attorney, but dismissed the idea. She hadn't been accused of anything, and she didn't want to give the impression that she thought she or

Nick had anything to hide. She prayed silently that she was right, that cooperation with the police was the best way to handle this situation.

"Well, I guess that would be all right."

Officer Morris, handcuffs dangling from her belt, strode in front of Anna, leading the way to a small office. "Please. Sit down."

Anna dropped into the seat indicated and waited for the woman to speak. The officer took her time arranging herself in her chair, then folding her arms under her breasts. She stared at Anna without an ounce of compassion in her eyes.

For a long minute, neither spoke, then Officer Morris said, "Your son has gotten himself in a lot of trouble, Mrs. Farmer. Has he ever been accused of a crime before?"

"No. Never," she replied, glad that at least she could truthfully say that.

"How's his behavior at school? Has he been in trouble there recently?"

Anna's heart sank. There was no way she could hide Nick's suspension from the police, but she could try to put the best spin on what had happened in October. "Nick was suspended from school for a week last fall. He led a student protest at the high school. A sit-in in the principal's office." She tried a laugh, but the sound rang false. "I guess I've raised a child of the sixties."

"Do you promote free sex in your family?"

"What?" She looked at the dark expression on the officer's face. The woman was serious!

"You said you've raised a child of the sixties. Weren't the sixties a time of increased sexual freedom?"

Anna felt her anger begin to assert itself. "No. That's not what I meant, and you know it. I was referring to the tactics Nick used to protest the unfair search and seizure that went on at the high school in early fall. He got the idea for a sit-in from Martin Luther King, not the hippies in Haight-Ashbury."

Her face flushed, Anna added, "My son is a good kid. I can't believe he would try to rape a girl. He has a steady girlfriend who he's been seeing for six months. Why would he take advantage of this girl at the party?"

The female officer's eyes bore into Anna. "I don't know, Mrs. Farmer. Why would he?"

Anna jumped up. "You're making the assumption that he's guilty. I know my son. He would never push himself on a girl. Now, I want to see him."

Officer Morris rose slowly. "The girl involved in this incident is only fourteen, Mrs. Farmer. She was found by one of our officers with no clothes on, lying in a bed crying. Your half-naked son was hanging over her, and now he won't answer any of our questions. You draw your own conclusions."

With the woman's words ringing in Anna's ears, she followed the officer into the corridor and down a narrow passage to the lock up. After searching her person and confiscating her handbag, a guard admitted her to an interrogation room. Nick sat in a chair, his head resting on his crossed arms. When he heard the door open, he looked up. "Mom!" He sprang from his seat.

She raced around the table and hugged him. She wanted so badly to believe that he hadn't been part of the tawdry scene described by the police officer. Holding him at arm's length, she said, "Look me in the eyes and tell me you didn't do what they're accusing you of, Nicholas. Tell me you didn't almost have sex with that little girl."

Anna waited for Nick's assertion that nothing illegal had happened. It didn't come. Instead, he broke away and turned an angry glare on her.

"If you want to believe some girl you never met before you even hear my side of the story, then you'd better leave right now. I'd rather stay in jail than go home with someone who has no faith in me."

Anna couldn't move. She and Nick had spent the last few months building a tentative trust between them. If she didn't support him now, it could destroy everything they had worked for. However, if he was guilty... Unable to even think of that possibility, she put the idea of Nick's culpability out of her mind altogether. "I'm going out there and try to straighten this whole thing out. I'll be back in a little bit."

It took more than an hour, but the police finally released Nick into her care. In the car, the two of them settled into an uncomfortable silence. Although she had convinced him to tell his side of the story to the police, Nick still had not explained to her exactly what had happened. She waited for him to open up, but he spent the short ride home looking out the window.

She tried to make sense of the facts she had managed to garner from the police, who had a lot more experience with this sort of thing than she did. But they believed Nick's accuser, Samantha Miller, and had tried to blame Anna for condoning what they saw as her son's inappropriate sexual behavior. Were they right? In her gut, she didn't believe Nick was capable of such an act of aggression, but if he was so blameless, why was he playing the misunderstood martyr—a role he had abused in the past to deflect her from the truth?

Anna desperately wished that Dr. Elliot had been in town. If there was ever a time she needed sound parenting advice, it was now. Was she doing the right thing by taking Nick's side? By supporting him, was she sending him the message that it was all right to lie and have sex with a minor, willing or not?

The moment she pulled the car into the driveway, Nick jumped out. He took the key chain from around his neck and unlocked the door. By the time Anna entered the foyer, he had already disappeared upstairs. She heard him slam his bedroom door and lock it.

Sighing, she tossed her keys on the sideboard and went into the kitchen to make herself a cup of hot tea. Even if she knew exactly the right thing to say to her son, he wouldn't listen to her. Not tonight. She'd get some sleep and try to make sense of everything in the morning.

Nick threw himself facedown on his bed, bunching his pillow under him and pounding it a few times. This had been the worst day of his life. First Kelly had dumped him for a dumb hockey player, then, when he was just trying to have some fun and forget his problems, a drunken girl had lied to the cops, and now he was in trouble for something he hadn't done. Screw her! And screw his mother for immediately assuming he was guilty. If Dad had still been alive, he would have believed his only son. His father would have known that Nick could never attack a girl that way.

Turning over onto his back, he stared at the shadows crisscrossing his ceiling. He could really use a cigarette right now. To hell with his mother. So what if she smelled the smoke? Could he get in any worse trouble than he was already in?

Leaning off the bed, he felt around on the floor for his backpack, but it wasn't there. *Shit!* He'd left it over at Bob's house. He didn't have his smokes.

Falling backwards, Nick tried to keep the tears he'd felt closing in all night from finally escaping. Then he remembered. Bob's friend Eric had been selling joints at a party in September. He'd bought a few to be cool, although he hadn't smoked weed before. He and Bob had shared one that night, and they'd had a lot of fun, laughing and pigging out on junk food. Then he'd met Kelly, who didn't approve of drugs, and he'd forgotten all about his stash.

A smile spread slowly across his face. There were still two joints left. He stood up and went to his closet to look for the baggie he had hidden in a pile of old shoes. He found it on the second go-through. Taking a book of matches from the pocket of a rumpled pair of jeans lying on the floor, he placed the matches beside the joints on his bedside table. He reached under his bed for the clamshell he used for an ashtray on the rare occasions he smoked in his room.

Nick carefully opened the baggie, lifting it to his nose and smelling the contents. Although the pot was more than six months old, it still smelled sweet and pungent. He removed the largest joint and placed it between his lips, then lit a match. He watched the tip burn brightly as he inhaled, holding the harsh smoke in his lungs as long as he could before exhaling. He immediately felt a buzz. Coughing to clear his lungs, he took another deep draw. This time he held the smoke in longer, savoring the way the drug seeped into his body and made every extremity tingle.

He watched a plume of smoke waft up toward the shadowy ceiling and started to giggle. He imagined how his mother would react if she came in and saw him. She had as much as accused him of being a criminal tonight, when he hadn't done anything wrong but drink a few beers. What would she think of him now that he really was breaking the law? Would she call the cops on him?

Nick finished the joint, stubbing it out in the shell. He pulled his shoes and socks off, then the rest of his clothes, letting them fall to the floor beside him. Drawing down the covers, he crawled into bed. Within minutes, he was fast asleep.

8

After returning with Nick from the police station, Anna had tried every trick in the book to make herself sleepy. Chamomile tea, hot milk, a warm bath—nothing had done the trick. She had barely slept a wink. Replays of the evening's events kept rolling through her consciousness. Even the few minutes of sleep she did experience were restless, her dreams filled with dark, formless shapes and angry, accusatory faces. Kevin's reassuring image, which had been appearing regularly in her dreams, did not materialize, as if he, too, were withholding judgment.

As soon as it was light out, Anna got up and dressed in her exercise clothes. Careful not to make a noise that might disturb her son, she tiptoed down the stairs and let herself out the front door.

She walked to the park entrance, trying to keep her mind open and savor the glory of the perfect spring day. The sky was clear and blue, with only a light breeze to whisper its presence amidst the gangly tree limbs and spreading shrubs. She could smell the richness of the damp earth and the special aroma of newborn leaves in the air. Just being out on such a wondrous day raised her spirits.

She took the now familiar path into the forest, her feet sure but her resolve faltering with every step. Her need to talk to Hawk was so overwhelming that she was afraid of what she might do if she didn't find him meditating on his rock. She had muddled through last night's trauma alone, but sensed that she had botched things badly. How ironic that she needed a dose of this child's wisdom to get her back on track.

There was only one thing Anna felt certain of this morning. What she did or said to Nick now would either strengthen or destroy the bridge they had slowly and painstakingly built between their two worlds over the fall and winter. She couldn't afford to screw up again.

When she heard the creek bubbling, she pulled up short, afraid that she would turn the corner and see that the rock was empty.

Nick watched his mother leave the house and head down the street for her morning walk. He waited a few minutes to make sure she wasn't just doing a loop of the development and coming back. When he was confident that she was really gone for a while, he picked up the phone and dialed Bob's cell number. After ten rings, his friend's groggy voice came on the line. "'lo?"

"Bob, it's me, Nick. Wake up!"

"Hang on."

Nick heard a rustling of sheets, footsteps fading into the distance, then, after a little bit, the flush of a toilet. Bob returned to the line. "Hey, what happened to you last night? We waited for you down the road a bit, but you never showed. You didn't get caught by the cops, did you?"

"I need to see you. Can you come over and pick me up?"

"Yeah, okay, later."

"No! Now. Something really bad happened last night. I need to talk to you about it. My mother is taking a walk. I want to get out of here before she comes back."

He heard a heavy sigh and then a grunt. "Okay. You can take me to Mickey D's for breakfast."

"Deal."

Anna almost sobbed with relief when she heard Hawk's gentle voice drifting on the spring breeze. "You can do it, Anna."

Without hesitation, she began to run, not even slowing down to find the narrowest place to ford the stream. Taking a long stride and pushing off from an exposed rock, she flew across the water, landing solidly on her feet on the other bank.

Hawk clapped his hands together and laughed. "Good going, Anna."

Smiling in spite of herself at the praise, she hopped up on the rock and took her accustomed place. It no longer amazed her that the spot was warm to the touch. She expected it to be.

They immediately fell into a comfortable silence, Anna closing her eyes and allowing the healing power of meditation and mindfulness to permeate her soul. At one point, she marveled at how easy it had become for her to move into a deeper state of relaxation and awareness. A little later in the meditation, a sense of gratitude swept through her, and she acknowledged how much the man-child sitting across from her had taught her in his own quiet way.

When she finally opened her eyes, she found Hawk smiling at her. "Thank you," he said, nodding his head slightly and placing his fisted hand over his heart.

She nodded back, convinced that he had entered her mind during their meditation and received her blessing. She didn't have to understand how he had accomplished the feat. She just knew he had done it.

They sat for a few minutes smiling at each other, then Anna said, "I need your advice."

"Do you?" Hawk tilted his head, a quizzical look on his face.

Anna ignored his question and plowed ahead, telling him how Nick had lied to her about going to an underage drinking party, and then a drunken fourteen-year-old girl had accused him of trying to force her into having sex with him.

Hawk cocked his head. "I don't understand. What do you want from me?"

"I want to know what I should say to Nick. Should I tell him that I trust him, that I know he's telling the truth, and no matter what happens, I love him?"

"Is that what you want to say?"

"I think so, but what if he did attack that girl? I can't let him think that I condone that kind of behavior."

Hawk shook his head, smiling ruefully. "Why do you have to give Nick a sermon every time he does something you don't like? Don't you think he understands that lying or taking advantage of a young girl is wrong?"

Anna shifted uncomfortably in her seat. She wasn't used to having a teenager lecture her.

"You've already taught Nick about honesty and integrity by modeling those values in your own life. He knows the difference between right and wrong. Hasn't he always treated girls with respect? He needs your support and guidance, not a class in morals. He'll learn from the natural consequences of his behaviors."

"So I should support him?"

"Follow your heart, and you won't go wrong."[46]

Anna felt a power greater than herself pulling her to her son. There were some things she had to clear up with him, and they couldn't wait. Hawk had reminded her that by listening to her heart she would always know how to be an effective, loving parent. Now she had to make certain Nick knew exactly what was in her heart. She stood abruptly, jumped off the rock, and headed home.

Once she let herself into the house, she climbed the stairs two at a time. She paused when she saw Nick's door hanging open. Peaking around the frame, she saw that he was gone. She rushed back downstairs and called to him from the basement door. When he didn't answer, she flipped on the light switch and went to check the playroom, although she knew he wouldn't be down there.

Her feet dragged as she made her way back to the kitchen and sat heavily in a chair. Staring out the window, she prayed that Nick hadn't done anything drastic, like run away. The after-effects of her morning meditation and talk with Hawk kept her from sinking into despair; still, she couldn't help but blame herself for causing this latest rift between them. Last night she had ignored the message of her heart, instead allowing her rational mind to take over. If she had been in Nick's shoes, she would have felt betrayed and angry, too. She just hoped their relationship wasn't permanently damaged.[47]

She needed Nick to come home. Soon.

The minutes dragged on. Anna had to do something to alleviate her anxiety. She decided to go upstairs to his room and investigate. Maybe he'd left a note or something.

With a renewed sense of purpose, she eagerly mounted the steps to the second floor. She entered Nick's room tentatively, as if he might jump out from the closet and accuse her of invading his private space without permission. Of course, nothing happened. After conducting a quick search of his room, she realized how silly she had been to jump to the conclusion that her son had run away. All his clothes that weren't heaped in piles on the floor were accounted for. Maybe one of his friends had called, and they had gone out to talk over the night's events.

Feeling a lot better, she sat on his bed. She absently picked up his pillow and held it to her chest. It smelled faintly of after-shave. Suddenly, a tear trickled down her cheek. Her little boy was gone. A teenager slept in this bed now. A fallible teenager who was doing the best he could to grow into his manhood. A wave of non-judgmental acceptance surged through her. How hard these last few years must have been on Nick without a father to look up to and guide him. How hard those same years had been on her without a husband to help her raise her son. A flash of insight took her breath away. She and Nick were both doing the best they could under less than optimal circumstances.

She wiped the tears from her face. As she turned to replace his pillow, her glance fell on the items sitting on Nick's night table. A plastic baggie with a hand-rolled cigarette, a pack of matches, and an ashtray with a partially smoked joint parked in it. Instead of putting his pillow back, she leaned over and buried her face in it. She didn't move even when she heard a car pull up outside the house and a door open and slam.

Nick was whistling to himself as he slipped his key in the lock. He was feeling better about the incident with the police. Although he might get in trouble for being at the party, Bob said he'd tell the police about the way the girl had come on to Nick and how she'd dragged him up the stairs, not the other way around. He thought Bob's eyewitness account might force Samantha to tell the truth.

He pushed the door to his room open and stopped in the doorway. His mother sat on his bed, not two feet from the joint and the roach he had smoked last night. Nick's good mood disappeared. She had to have seen the drug paraphernalia. He had just gotten himself out of shit, and now he had stepped in it again.

"Mom. What are you doing in here?" he asked. He walked toward her, determined to stay cool no matter what. To his surprise, she didn't say anything. She dropped the pillow she'd been holding and stood up. She took a few steps toward him. He refused to retreat. He stood his ground, waiting for the tirade to start. Instead of yelling at him, his mother reached out and hugged him. "I know you're doing the best you can, Nick. I'm sorry I didn't act like I trusted you last night, but I do. You're not the kind of person to force himself on anyone. I know you would never have hurt that girl."

He was so relieved that his mother wasn't mad at him that he let her hug him for a long time. He even hugged back, and it didn't feel uncomfortable. He couldn't remember a time when he had enjoyed—or needed—a hug as much as he did this one. Not that his mother had tried to hug him much. He hadn't been the most lovable kid recently.

When they broke apart, Nick put his arm around his mother's shoulders. "Let's go downstairs and talk. I want to tell you what really happened yesterday."

Anna smiled inwardly. Her son was trying to pull a fast one, hoping to distract her so she wouldn't notice the pot by his bedside. Not that there was a chance in hell that anyone with half a brain could have missed it.

"I'd rather talk in here, if you don't mind." She retraced her steps and sat down on the bed. Nick came over and placed himself between her and the marijuana.

He outlined Friday's disasters, beginning with his problems with Kelly and ending with Samantha's whopper of a lie. Anna listened intently. Her son's words rang with sincerity. Then he told her about going out to breakfast with Bob and how his friend had agreed to go to the police to support his story.

"I wish there was a way to keep the police out of all this. Although I know you're telling the truth, and Bob's testimony might help, there's still a good chance that Samantha could convince a judge or jury that you tried to rape her. I wish I knew what her motivation for lying was."

"Maybe she was afraid of getting in trouble with her parents." Nick rubbed his left temple. "Do you think if we called her house and talked to her folks or went over there to confront her, she'd admit she was lying and drop the charges?"

"I'm not sure. Let me think about it a little." Anna stood up and walked to the door. Before she left the room, she turned and said in her calmest voice, "Oh, by the way, Nick. This is a drug-free and a smoke-free house."

She watched his face turn bright red. "I know, Mom." He picked up the baggie and offered it to her. "Here. Take this. Last night was only the second time I tried weed. I'm really not into drugs."

Anna took the plastic bag and folded it into her pocket. "You're a smart kid, Nick. I know you don't need me to lecture you about how drugs are illegal, or about underage drinkers going to parties where liquor is served, or lying to your mother about where you're going."

He looked at his feet. "I screwed up, Mom. I'm sorry."

"I know you are, Nick. I know this has been a difficult time for you. I'm sure it won't happen again."

"It won't, Mom."

She went to the bathroom and flushed the joint down the toilet, then stripped and got into the shower.[48]

Later in the day, Nick rode his bike over to Allison's house so she could help him study for a Spanish test. Anna was in the basement checking on the seedlings she had been growing under lights since January when she heard the phone. She rushed upstairs, catching it on the fourth ring.

"Hello," she said breathlessly.

"Mrs. Farmer?" a tentative female voice asked.

"Yes, this is she. Can I help you?"

"My name is Mary Miller. My daughter, Samantha, is the girl your son was with last night."

For a moment, anger welled up inside Anna. This woman's child had lied about Nick to the police and could ruin his life. Then, just as quickly as it came, her anger subsided. Talking to Mary Miller was exactly what Nick had suggested they do. She took a deep breath and completely let go of her resentments and preconceived negative assumptions. When she felt centered and in control again, she spoke. "Hello, Mary. I'm glad you called."

The mothers quickly warmed to each other. When Anna explained Nick's side of the story, she was relieved to find that Mrs. Miller believed her daughter was lying, also.

"Her father is a strict disciplinarian. Samantha is more afraid of him coming down hard on her than she is about being caught in a lie. To tell you the truth, I'm at my wits end. She's been a real handful recently, and I don't know how to handle her."

By the end of their conversation, they had arranged to bring Nick to the Miller's the following day and confront Samantha with the truth. Mrs. Miller assured Anna that, once her daughter understood the severe consequences that Nick faced because of her, she would do the right thing.

When Nick returned from Allison's, Anna sat down with him and told him about her conversation with Mary Miller. He readily agreed to the plan the two mothers had worked out.

As long as he was so receptive and cooperative, Anna decided to gather up her courage and bring up another topic. "Nick, I haven't wanted you to know this, but things are really getting bad at work. Gerry is planning to lay off half the creative staff, and he'll probably dump even more work in my lap over the next few months."

"Then why don't you quit, Mom? Gerry's an asshole. He doesn't deserve to have someone great like you to do his dirty work."

Surprised and honored by her son's belief in her, Anna couldn't keep a pleased smile off her face. "You mean, you knew—"

"Mom, it doesn't take a degree in psychology to figure out you hate your job. Why don't you try to get work as a landscape designer? That's what you really love doing, isn't it?"

Anna's heart filled with unconditional love for her son. They really were a lot alike. His words echoed exactly what she had been thinking. "As a matter of fact, I've been looking around. I already went to a couple of interviews but, so far, no one has called to offer me a job."

"That's okay, Mom. I'm sure you'll get something soon."

Frowning slightly, she looked up at her son. "Nick, if I do quit Gerry's, we'll probably have to move. Jobs in horticulture can be seasonal, and they don't pay nearly as well as office work."

"I don't care. This house is too big for just the two of us, anyway. We could move into an apartment or something. Now that the two high schools have merged, we can live anywhere in the township, and I won't have to switch schools."

Anna sat in stunned silence. She had lost her kind-hearted little boy when he'd turned thirteen, but she now saw before her a glimpse of the good-hearted man he was destined to become. They still had a bumpy road to travel together before he graduated from high school and moved out on his own, but she was willing to put up with the setbacks knowing they were moving forward more often than backwards.

She smiled at her son. "Thanks, Nick. Knowing how you feel will help me make my decision."

They both stood. Nick turned to her and gave her a hug. "Don't worry, Mom. Everything will be all right. I'll help with money. I'll get an afternoon job." He broke off the hug and held up his palm. "Deal?"

She slapped his open hand. "Deal."

The following morning, Anna drove the two of them to the Miller's house. The impressive Tudor-style mansion sat on several acres of land overlooking the reservoir.

Mrs. Miller met them at the front door and ushered them into a formal living room decorated with white French provincial furniture and white shag carpeting. A white baby grand piano stood in the bow window. Anna sat on the uncomfortable couch, Nick claiming the seat right next to her.

Mrs. Miller hovered over them, her hands clasping and unclasping in front of her. "Would you like something to drink? I think there's some iced tea in the fridge."

Anna shook her head. She looked over at Nick, who also declined.

"Then let me go and find Sam. I think she's down in the game room. I won't be but a minute." The thin, nervous woman disappeared through the doorway.

Anna felt Nick squirm next to her. "This place gives me the creeps," he whispered in her ear.

"Me, too." She didn't know what else to say to alleviate his obvious nervousness, so they sat together in silence until they heard voices coming closer.

"Why did you make me stop playing? You know *Snood* is my favorite game."

"We have guests, Samantha. People you need to talk to."

The pair appeared in the doorway, Mrs. Miller with her arm wrapped tightly around her daughter's shoulders. The girl took one look at Nick, and her face turned bright red. She tried to turn and leave, but her mother held her firmly. "This is important, Sam. You have to face up to what happened Friday night. You have to tell the truth."

Samantha turned on her mother, fire shooting from her eyes. "You don't believe me? You'd believe a complete stranger over your own daughter? That's great, Mom. Just great."

Anna rose from the sofa. She smiled and held out her hand. "Hello, Samantha. My name is Anna. Nick is my son."

The girl shot Anna a quick glance, hesitated a moment, then reluctantly shook hands.

The non-accusatory way Anna greeted the young girl broke the ice. Samantha slouched into an overstuffed armchair and waited.

Anna continued. "Nick and I are here to talk to you about what happened Friday night, not because we're mad at you or want to blame you for anything, but because my son's story is a little different from yours. Your mom thought that, since your dad left for a business trip this morning, you might be willing to talk more frankly about the incident."

They waited. Samantha pulled a thread from the chair's arm.

"Sam, please. The furniture." Her mother sent the girl a stern look.

Samantha stopped picking at the fabric, but began to kick her feet into the white carpet. No one could fail to hear the exasperated sigh that escaped from her mother's lips.

"I'd really like to hear from you what happened at the party Friday night, Sam. Won't you please tell us? I don't care if it's not exactly what you told the police." Anna stared at the girl, who kept her gaze on the carpet. "This is really serious. My son could go to jail for a long time if you don't tell the truth. Is that what you want, Sam? To be responsible for having Nick locked up and his whole life destroyed because you're afraid of your father?"

Samantha darted a remorseful look at Anna, then threw a side-ways glance in Nick's direction. Anna held her breath, hoping and praying that the girl would see the fear and sadness in his eyes and understand what her lies were doing to him.

After a few moments of tense silence, the girl began to speak so softly that Anna had to lean over to hear her. "I kind of made a mistake. I drank too much at the party." She cast a glance in her mother's direction. Mrs. Miller nodded, encouraging her daughter to continue. "I was acting really stupid." She looked shyly at Nick. "I guess I pushed myself on you. I thought you were some other guy I met earlier."

Anna felt triumphant. The nightmare was almost over.

Without looking up, the girl continued. "My father wants me to be perfect. He's really strict." She turned to her mother, her voice quivering, on the brink of tears. "Neither of you knows anything about who I really am. You don't want to know because then you'd be disappointed because I'm not perfect."

Before Mrs. Miller could respond, Anna leaned over and placed her hand on the girl's. "Growing up is hard, isn't it, Samantha?"

She sniffled back a sob and nodded.

"I'm sure you're doing the best you can, to grow up, I mean." She looked over at Nick and smiled. "Things will get better. I promise."

To Anna's surprise, Nick joined in the conversation. "Your parents are probably doing the best that they can, too, you know. Kids can make their parents' lives miserable when they want to. I should know. I'm an expert."

For the first time since she entered the room, Samantha kept her gaze elevated. A small smile crept across her mouth. "Yeah."

By the time Anna and Nick were ready to head home, the police had been called and the pending investigation dropped. Nick and Samantha would still have to appear before a local magistrate and pay a fine for underage drinking, but the crisis had been averted.

At the door, Nick spoke a few encouraging words to Samantha. Anna hugged Mrs. Miller.

"You handled this whole thing so beautifully, Anna. I'd love to take you to lunch sometime and pick your brain. Maybe some of your wisdom would rub off on me."

Anna laughed. "I could write a book about all the dramas Nick and I have put each other through."

"Yeah," agreed Nick. "That could be your new job, Mom. Writing a book about how to keep teenagers and their parents from driving each other crazy."

They waved goodbye and got in the Saab. Anna put the car in gear and pulled out of the driveway. She drove on automatic pilot, her mind returning repeatedly to Nick's words. *You should write a book, Mom.* Why not? Why not write about her struggles to become a better parent so that others could learn from her mistakes and triumphs? Why the heck not?

They drove for a while in silence. Then Nick asked, "Can you drop me off at Bob's? I told him I'd hang out with him after we finished talking to Samantha and her mother."

Anna took a moment to ponder Nick's request in the light of recent events. "I don't know, Nick. You haven't exactly been a poster child for responsible behavior this weekend. Since you lied to me about hanging out at Bob's house Friday night and were drinking and smoking marijuana, I'm not sure I can trust you."

"Come on, Mom. I said I was sorry. I really screwed up. I won't do it again. Promise."

"Maybe this is a good place to start rebuilding trust between us. Tell me, Nick. What can you do to help rebuild my trust in you?"

"I don't know. Stop lying. Tell you where I'm going."

"That's a good start, but it's not quite enough." Anna paused for a moment, then continued. "How would you feel if we made a deal? For now, you can go over to friends' houses as long as I talk to the parents first."

Nick looked at her from under his thick eyelashes. "How long is 'for now'?"

"For however long it takes for us to build trust again—it could be a year, it could be a month. That's up to you. Do you think that makes sense?"

"Yeah, I guess."

Despite the grudging tone in his voice and the way he slouched down in his seat, Nick was obviously relieved that she hadn't grounded him for his misbehavior. Anna felt good about the way she had handled things. By placing the responsibility for his behavior in Nick's lap, she had removed herself from the role of disciplinarian. If he screwed up, it would take longer to win back her trust. If he did okay, the consequence vanished.[49,50]

9

Too restless to stay home and clean her house, her usual Sunday routine, Anna changed into her walking gear and hurried to the park. Before heading down the steep hill on the path that led to the creek, she adjusted her stride to make sure she had good traction. So much had happened since she last visited Hawk that she could barely believe it had only been yesterday.

His advice to "follow your heart" had seen her through what could have been the worst day of her life as a parent. She couldn't wait to tell him that Nick's accuser had dropped the attempted rape charge because, as a mother-son team, they had worked together to convince the Miller girl to do the right thing. Even the way they'd negotiated the consequences for Nick's irresponsible actions Friday night had been civil, and both of them had come out of it feeling that justice had been served. If anything, Nick respected her more than ever because of the way she had handled herself, staying present and not allowing herself to be caught up in his teenage drama.

Her success was still so new to her that Anna had a hard time believing the changes she had made in herself would stick. She thought she still needed Hawk to remind her of what was important in life, to challenge her when she fell down.

She heard the bubbling of the stream and smiled expectantly, trying to remember the crippled woman who had hidden in the bushes months ago, afraid of the power wielded by a wise youth with extraordinary perceptiveness.

Turning the corner, she stopped abruptly. Her heart rose in her throat and disappointment choked her. The meditation rock was empty. Her disappointment veered dangerously close to anger before Anna stopped herself. Instead of taking Hawk's absence as a personal affront, the way the old Anna would have, she inhaled deeply and reminded herself to let go of expectations, to stay in the present and not judge Hawk for being somewhere else when she wanted to see him.

She scrambled across the brook on the back of the downed tree. Just because Hawk wasn't there didn't mean she couldn't sit on the rock and meditate by herself. If there was one thing she had learned during the previous months it was to enjoy her own company.

When she hoisted herself onto the rock, she saw it—the green carved dragon amulet on the chain that Hawk always wore. Beside the necklace was a piece of neatly-folded paper addressed to her. Before she touched the medallion, she opened the note and read the simple message: "Accept and appreciate every precious moment, Anna."

She picked up the amulet. As she placed the chain carefully around her neck, she felt a golden glow saturate her whole body. Instead of sitting in her customary position, her back to the rushing water, she took Hawk's spot. Assuming the meditation position she had learned from her young mentor, she focused on the passage of air through her nostrils. As random thoughts entered her mind, she simply observed the beginning, middle, and end of the thought. Then she gently but firmly refocused her attention back to her breath.

She sat on the rock meditating, relaxing, letting a deep sense of peace come over her. When she was satisfied with her level of relaxation, she opened her eyes and stretched her arms over her head. She felt wonderful. When she stood up and turned to let the late afternoon sun warm her face, a ray fell directly across her chest, hitting the multi-faceted dragon carving and sending warmth back out into the atmosphere.

Anna made her way home in a leisurely fashion, fingering the amulet around her neck, a smile lingering on her lips.

When she got home, she took off Hawk's amulet, leaving it on top of the radiator where she always put her keys. Feeling too peaceful and happy to waste her time doing boring housework, she grabbed a pad and pencil and sat down at the kitchen table to start planning her book. She had only written one sentence when the phone rang. She was tempted to let it go, but something compelled her to get up and answer it.

"Hello, Anna? It's Charles Southeby calling."

She thought her heart would jump out of her chest. She swallowed hard and said, "Yes, Charles. How are you?"

"I'm fine, especially since the board of the Historic Trust has made a decision about hiring a new groundskeeper and apprentice gardener. I'm calling to offer you the position."

Anna swallowed again. "And the caretaker's cottage?"

"Goes along with the job rent free, young lady."

Anna wanted to shout with glee. She contained herself long enough to accept the offer and arrange a few details with the very proper Charles Southeby. Once he had rung off, however, she yelled and screamed to her heart's content. She tried calling Carol, but she wasn't home. She thought about picking up Nick at Bob's, but decided that she would probably embarrass him in front of his friend, so she refrained.

She sat at the kitchen table and sipped cup after cup of chamomile tea, which, unfortunately, did nothing to calm her nerves. Every ten minutes she speed-dialed Carol until her friend finally answered. Carol was ecstatic over the good news and promised to stop by later that evening with a split of champagne to celebrate.

Even after chatting with her friend, Anna still couldn't stop thinking about her incredible good fortune. She would have to put the house on the market immediately, since she and Nick would be moving into the caretaker's cottage on the property of the historic Woolrich House in three weeks. Three weeks and her new life would begin. And best of all, she could go into work tomorrow and tell Gerry to put his head where his heart was: up his you know what!

She looked at the blank paper in front of her. The next days would be hectic, but there was nothing she could do about it right now. Before she squandered the rest of the afternoon on flights of fancy, she needed to refocus on her work.

She picked up her pencil and wrote her working title on the top of the first page: *Finding the Path: A Handbook for Parents of Teenagers.* She had no doubt the title would change before the book was published, but it was a start. She placed numbers in the left margin from one to six, spaced evenly apart, then she began to write down the essential points she wanted her book to include.

1. Look at your own shortcomings before blaming, criticizing, or judging your child. You are helping your teenager when you help yourself. A teenager learns more from how you live your life than from what you say. Modeling healthy behavior works better than lecturing. Rather than projecting your own shortcomings onto your child and judging him or her, look in the mirror. See those aspects of yourself that you don't like and make the necessary steps to change them.

2. To be an effective parent, you must be pro-active rather than reactive. Before jumping in to argue, mete out a punishment, or express anger or hurt at your teenager's words or behaviors, take the time to ask yourself, "What is my goal here?" Healthy goals include: teaching responsibility and accountability, increasing independence, and developing greater empathy and feelings of love. Unhealthy goals include: winning a power struggle, proving that you're right and your teen is wrong, and keeping your child dependent on you.

3. Step back from the drama and stress that a teenager—especially an oppositional one—brings into your life by practicing meditation

or other forms of mindfulness. This practice will help you keep sight of the larger picture.

4. Natural and logical consequences of your child's inappropriate behaviors are focused on the present or in the future and are more effective than punishment, which is revengeful and focused on the past.

5. The teen years are a time of unparalleled growth for your child (and you). As the parent of an aspiring adult, you must let go of your role as primary teacher and forge a new, at times collegial, relationship with your teen. Parents must encourage and help their teens find their own solutions, allowing them to make mistakes and learn from them.

6. The most important lesson parents of teenagers must learn: follow your heart. Come at the problems and challenges your children throw at you daily from a place of love, not fear. Before lashing out at your often emotional, irrational teen, put yourself in your child's shoes. What is it like for him right now? Is he doing the best he can under the circumstances?

Anna paused to reread what she had written. She was about halfway done when she heard the front door open. "Nick. Can you come in the kitchen for a minute? I have something to tell you."

Dropping the CDs Bob had burned for him on the dining room table, Nick went into the kitchen. "What's up?" he asked as he headed for the refrigerator to get himself a glass of milk.

"I got a job offer today."

His hand on the handle of the refrigerator, he spun around and shot her a questioning look. "And?"

"And I'm going to take it."

Forgetting about his thirst, Nick strode to his mother's side and lifted her out of her chair, crushing her in a bear hug. "Tell me everything."

"I will if you let me go."

They sat at the table together while she filled him in on the job and their new home on the Woolrich estate.

"Sounds great, Mom."

Nick looked around the comfortable kitchen in the house he had grown up in. Now that there was no doubt that they'd be moving, and soon, he suddenly felt sad. This house held memories of what their family had been like when his father was still alive, when Nick had had a man in his life to help him through tough times. He loved his mother, and he respected how hard she was working to be a good parent these days, but she couldn't take the place of his father.

"You look sad. Does it bother you that we're leaving this house?"

"Kind of. It's the memories of Dad, I think, though, not the place itself. I really miss him."

His mother fell silent. When she spoke, he could hear her voice choked with emotion. "Yeah. It's hard to let go of the past, but we'll always have memories of Dad no matter where we move. As long as we're alive, he'll be alive inside us."

"I know. But I wish..." He let his voice trail off. He didn't want to be disloyal to his father's memory or hurt his mother.

"What?" his mother asked in a gentle voice.

"I wish I had some older guy in my life to take me to ball games and do the stuff Dad did with me."

"I'm sorry I haven't been able to find a strong male role model for you, Nick."

"Hey, it's not your fault. I was just thinking that I might sign up for the mentoring program that Ms. Blackmun told me about."

"The one where a faculty member acts like an advisor and after-school big brother or big sister?"

Nick looked up. "You remember?"

She smiled at him. "Sure. And I think it's a great idea."

He sat up straighter and smiled back. "Cool. There's this neat teacher who got transferred from Lincoln this fall. I have him for speech, but he's also the drama coach. He asked me to be on the crew for the spring musical, and I said I would. Tech crew has to report tomorrow night from seven to ten." He hesitated, a touch of uncertainty in his eyes. "Is that okay, Mom? For me to be on the crew? It will mean you'll have to drive me back and forth to school two or three nights a week."

Anna smiled to reassure her son. "Of course it's okay."

He grinned back at her. "Anyway, Mr. Matula might be willing to be my mentor. Maybe I'll ask him tomorrow."

"I think that's a great idea, Nick."

Her tall, lanky son stood up. Leaning over, he kissed her on the cheek. "Congratulations, Mom. I know you're going to be great at the new job."

Trying hard to keep the tears out of her eyes, Anna replied, "Thanks, buddy."

As she dressed for work the next morning, Anna found that she was both nervous and excited. She had waited a long time to tell her blustery, unpleasant boss that she no longer needed his lousy job, but she was still scared of his sharp tongue and what he would say to her when she gave him her notice.

Although her fingers trembled so badly she had trouble buttoning her blouse, she had never felt more certain that she had chosen the right path.

"Bye, Mom," she heard Nick call to her from the front door. "Good luck with Gerry."

"Thanks, kiddo. I'll need it," she replied. "Have a great day in school."

The door slammed and Nick was gone.

A few minutes later, Anna slipped her coat on and reached for her keys, accidentally knocking Hawk's amulet onto the floor. She stooped to pick it up, cradling it in her palm and feeling the stone's warmth spread through her body. Standing, she closed her fingers around the warm stone, held it tightly to her chest, and closed her eyes. An image of Hawk's smiling eyes filled her consciousness. She could hear his soft voice telling her, "You can do it, Anna." Once she had absorbed all the magic the amulet had to offer her, she put it down almost reverently and headed out the door.

Arriving at the office at eight, hoping to get to Gerry before the busy day began, she barely had time to take off her jacket and start a pot of coffee before he buzzed her.

"We have a crisis. Get in here right away."

She shook her head at the man's rudeness. He hadn't even addressed her by her name.

Pushing her hair behind her ears nervously, she grabbed a steno pad and walked down the corridor to his office. A small smile played over her lips when she saw the condition of the room. Thanks to all the firings he had initiated recently, the boss man was having to do some of the creative work himself, and it looked like he was losing control.

"What are you smiling at?" he barked, sending her one of his condescending scowls. "If you were doing your job, this place wouldn't be such a hell hole."

Anna pursed her lips, but she didn't let him get a rise out of her. "I'm glad you mentioned my job, Gerry, because there's something I have to tell you."

"It can wait. Upland Oil called again—"

Anna slapped her pad down on a clean corner of his desk.

Gerry looked up, his face wreathed in surprise. "What the—"

Anna straightened her spine. "This can't wait, Gerry. I'm giving you two weeks notice. I'm quitting."

"What? Is this some ploy to get a raise?"

"No, Gerry. I'm leaving. If you want me to put an ad in the paper for my replacement, I'll do it as soon as we're done here."

"You can't leave. There's too much work to do, and you haven't been pulling your share of the load recently."

Despite her resolve to remain calm, she couldn't let a bold-faced lie go unanswered. "How much is my share of the load, Gerry? Two hundred percent?"

He sat back in his chair and smiled. "You do want more money, don't you? Well, okay, I can give you a raise. How much would make you happy?"

"I'll say this one more time, Gerry. I'm leaving. Now, do you want to talk about Upland or not?"

She watched his face turn an unhealthy shade of red. "Never mind the Upland account. Put the ad in the paper and then get the hell out of here. You're fired."

Anna dropped the pad on Gerry's desk, turned on her heels, and walked slowly to the door. Before she left, she faced him and said, "Don't worry, I'm leaving, but you can't fire me, Gerry. I already resigned, remember?"

Taking advantage of her newfound freedom, Anna met Nick at the bus stop, and they drove over to look at the cottage on the Woolrich estate. Feeling as if a huge yoke had been removed from around her neck, Anna splurged on a celebratory dinner for the two of them at the local steak house. She dropped him off at play rehearsal at seven, then went home to work on her book some more. At ten, she was back at school, waiting outside the auditorium entrance with the other parents. Anna felt a sense of pride in Nick, not for any outward accomplishment that made her look good as a parent, but for the interesting, independent young man he was becoming.

Nick was one of the last students to leave the building. Whereas in the past Anna would have been furious at him for dragging his heels and worried that he had done something wrong, tonight she waited patiently, not allowing herself to go to a place of fear or anger. Eventually, he emerged from the building with a nice-looking man dressed casually in jeans and a College of Santa Fe sweatshirt. Nick brought him over to the car, and Anna rolled her window down. "Mom, this is Mr. Matula—I mean, Tony."

The man, whose dark hair was just beginning to show streaks of gray at the temples, leaned forward to shake Anna's hand. "You've got a great son here, Mrs. Farmer. Nick mentioned that he'd like me to be his mentor. If it's all right with you, I'd be happy to take on the assignment."

Anna smiled. She liked Mr. Tony Matula. Her intuition told her he was a good man. "Anyone who has my son's best interests at heart is okay with me. You and Nick can work out the details."

On the ride home, Nick chatted excitedly about the things he'd learned from Tony and the student who headed the tech crew. "Tony thinks I might end up being in charge of lights because I'm so good with electronics, but I really want to learn how to construct sets. You should see how good some of the kids are who have the leads in the play. You're going to come to all three nights, aren't you, Mom?"

Anna laughed. "I don't know, son. Maybe I could swing it."

She pulled the car into the driveway and got out. "You're so wired you'll probably never get to sleep. Want me to make you a cup of tea or some hot milk?"

"Yeah, sure. I'll have some of that peppermint tea. I'm going to call Bob and see if I can get him to join the crew, then I'll be down."

Anna whistled almost as loudly as the kettle. Today had been one of the happiest days of her life. She thought how ironic that was. Adversity had been her constant companion for the four long years of her widowhood, yet everything that had happened in that period—her terrible grief, her constant fighting with Nick, her job woes, which had caused such terrible stress in her life—had been blessings in disguise. She had never felt more connected to the universe and at peace with herself than she did right now.[51]

She poured two cups of mint tea into mugs and put some cookies on a plate. Sitting at the table, she sipped her tea and waited for her son.

A tall, lanky figure with the shoulders of a man appeared in the doorway. Back lit by the bright hall light, his face was in shadow, but the green stone amulet he wore around his neck stood out against the white background of his T-shirt.

"Hawk, is that you?" she asked, confused about how the teen had gotten into her house.

Nick emerged from the shadows, his familiar face awash in the warm glow of the kitchen chandelier, his eyes smiling down at her. "What's the matter, Mom? Don't you recognize your own son?"

Anna shook her head to clear her mind. She had never tuned in to the extraordinary similarities between the teens' body types before, probably because Hawk was so dark and Nick was fair.

Nick sat next to her, the medallion gripped tightly in his hand. Anna stared at his hand, wondering when Nick had started sprouting hair on his knuckles. When had her little boy become a man?

"Where'd this necklace come from?" he asked, opening his fingers to show her the stone.

Anna reached out and touched it with her index finger. "Pretty cool, isn't it?"

"Actually, it's kind of hot to the touch. It makes my fingers tingle."

He took the necklace off and handed it to her. Anna stared at the green stone, and a realization hit her with the force of a sharp blow, almost taking her breath away. Hawk was gone. She would never see him again. The youth had come to her when she needed a spiritual guide, and now that she'd found her own path, he had moved out of her life forever.

"Mom? Are you okay? You look like you just saw a ghost."

Anna shook off her sadness. She refused to dwell on her loss, preferring instead to celebrate her new relationship with her growing son. She looked into Nick's smiling eyes and pushed the amulet back to him. "I want you to have this, son. I think it was meant for you, not me."

"Gee, thanks." He put it on. "Where'd you get it?"

"An amazing person—someone who reminds me a lot of you—gave it to me, and I think it's about time I told you about him. His name is Hawk."[52]

Appendix

I

Parent's Bill of Rights

1. I have the right to be treated with respect.
2. I have the right to take the time necessary to think through a decision or consequence with regards to my teen.
3. I have the right to make mistakes.
4. I have the right to make decisions for my teen that I believe are in her best interest.
5. I have the right to talk about my teen with other adults who may be able to help with his behavior and emotional and physical health.
6. I have the right to set and enforce rules to insure the safety of my teen.
7. I have the right to restrict my teen from spending time with adults and others whom I believe to be a negative influence.
8. I have the right to discipline my teen in ways that promote healthy behavior without compromising her emotional well-being.

9. I have the right to expect my teen to contribute to the general upkeep of the house in order to keep our home a pleasant environment in which to live.
10. I have the right to talk with the parents of my teen's friends and know my teen's whereabouts when she is away from home.
11. I have the right to privacy.

Appendix
II

Teenager's Bill of Rights

1. I have the right to be treated with respect.
2. I have the right to be treated humanely in regard to punishment.
3. I have the right to make mistakes.
4. I have the right to make my own age-appropriate choices.
5. I have the right to be acknowledged and praised for my efforts in becoming independent, responsible, and loving.
6. I have the right to be loved, nurtured and cared for regardless of how angry, hurt or confused I am.
7. I have the right to my own individuality in regard to how I dress, my religious beliefs, and my likes and dislikes.
8. I have the right to privacy.
9. I have the right to choose my own friends, especially as I get older.
10. I have the right to be included in decisions that will affect me, especially in school, at work, and in relationships.

Appendix

III

Parent's Responsibilities

1. It is my responsibility to provide love, nurturance, food, clothing, and shelter for my teen regardless of how angry I feel.
2. It is my responsibility to help my teen learn to make his own decisions and become independent from me.
3. It is my responsibility to allow my teen to experience the consequences of his behavior without being over-protective.
4. It is my responsibility to take care of myself and my own needs.
5. It is my responsibility to maintain my role as the adult, not take out my problems on my teen, and seek help for myself when I need it.
6. It is my responsibility to get my emotional needs met in other ways than through my teen, and to do what is best for him.
7. It is my responsibility to learn and use healthy, effective approaches to parenting my teen.
8. It is my responsibility to hug my teen when he needs a hug, challenge him when he needs to be challenged, listen to him when he

needs an ear, praise him for his efforts, and give him space when he needs it.

9. It is my responsibility to set and enforce age-appropriate limits and boundaries with my teen.

10. It is my responsibility to seek out and advocate an appropriate education for my teen that fits his learning needs.

11. It is my responsibility to seek out and provide appropriate academic, emotional, social and spiritual support for my teen when necessary.

Appendix

IV

Teenager's Responsibilities

1. It is my responsibility to treat my parents with the same level of respect that I expect from them.
2. It is my responsibility to seek out help in resolving problems I cannot handle on my own.
3. It is my responsibility to do my homework and participate in school.
4. It is my responsibility to pick up after myself and contribute to keeping the house clean and making it an enjoyable place to live.
5. It is my responsibility to learn to become independent from my parents and not expect them to do for me what I can do for myself, such as waking up in the morning, making my meals, doing my laundry, and washing my dishes.
6. It is my responsibility to choose friends who will be a positive influence on me, encouraging me to act in responsible ways that will contribute to my emotional and physical health.
7. It is my responsibility to take care of my body.

8. It is my responsibility to cooperate with those who are trying to help me and let them know in a respectful way if their actions are unhelpful or hurtful.
9. It is my responsibility to let my parents or a responsible adult know if anyone has hurt me in any way.
10. It is my responsibility to love and accept others and myself and not judge those who are different from me.

ENDNOTES

Chapter One

1 Nick's comment is very similar to a comment Anna made earlier to the police officer, but Anna does not see in her behavior a model for Nick's anti-authority behavior. Anna is not yet aware that she has issues with authority.

2 *You get what you expect.* Parents and children often "pigeon-hole" each other and make snap judgments based on previous patterns of behavior. Here, an attempt by Anna to change old patterns (e.g., to act with greater compassion and understanding) is quickly discounted as insincere by Nick, who has reason to distrust his mother's intentions. To avoid sounding judgmental and accusatory, instead of asking, "What am I bailing you out for this time?" Anna could have simply stated, "Tell me what happened." Even an accusatory tone of voice can trigger a teen's negative reaction to a parent's words.

3 Parents can take too much responsibility for their child's behavior. Although they are very important in their child's social and moral development-particularly in the younger years-the media, schooling, personal experiences, knowledge, and peer groups also influence behavior. Feeling guilty for not being perfect parents does nothing to help the situation and typically adds tension to the relationship.

4 Should the school punish Nick for his behavior? If so, what would it accomplish? When a teen is punished for expressing his anger and hurt, he can misperceive these expressions of emotion as being "wrong," leading to difficulties expressing feelings, or even identifying them, as an adult. Modeling healthy ways of expressing feelings, then coaching the adolescent in this process, will be more productive than punishing him.

5 Children who hold onto anger at their parents often generalize these feelings and project them onto other authority figures, becoming overly sensitive to those who have power over them. This is a major reason why so many children have "authority issues." Teens who have little tolerance for perceived injustice run into many difficulties because life is inherently not always "fair."

6   Anna is afraid other parents are judging her for her son's actions because she sees Nick's behaviors as a reflection of her parental worthiness. She is ignoring the many other influences on young adults (personality type, peer group, schooling, environment, experiences, etc.). By not taking Nick's behavior personally, Anna will be in a better position to respond objectively and, thus, effectively to his misbehavior.

7   It is normal for teens to want more privacy and power over their own lives as they mature, and they are more likely to share their experiences with parents they perceive to be supportive rather than invasive. Parents can help their teen towards independence without giving up their parental role by redefining the relationship from more authoritative to more democratic.

8   Anna became very angry with Nick because she knew he was going to turn the radio up, and she saw his act as a direct attempt to annoy her. When kids express anger at their parents, it is usually because they themselves are feeling angry. Sensing that Nick was ready to explode, Anna could have tried to diffuse his anger, rather than feeding into it with her own. For example, before driving away, she might have taken a "time out" and simply stated that she knew he was upset and that she was upset too. By reassuring him that she loved him and by offering to resolve the issue later when neither of them was mad, she could have avoided the heated altercation and hurtful words that followed.

9   It is important for parents to realize that their teen is also afraid of the struggle that leads to independence. One minute the teen wants her parents out of her life; the next she wants Dad to make lunch or Mom to drive her to the mall. Parents must avoid giving in to a child's dependency needs in order to satisfy their own emotional needs. For example, a mother who makes her 16-year-old lunch every day is not supporting independence; instead, she may be attempting to hang on to an unrealistic, overly dependent relationship.

Chapter Two

10 Most parents feel less than perfect in their parenting and may resent some aspect of it, such as Anna's feeling that she is too busy being a provider to be a good parent. The perfect parent does not exist. The struggles that parents and their children endure can be seen as opportunities rather than roadblocks.

11 Corporal punishment and strict discipline don't work with today's children who have become desensitized to the harsh hand of an authoritarian parent. Democratic approaches to parenting, which respect the child as an individual as well as a son or daughter and include him or her in the process of discipline, have always been more effective in raising healthy, productive and happy adults. We often use the same form of discipline used on us, especially if we believe we came out okay, denying such

founded truths as violence begets violence. Hitting children models physical violence as an appropriate way to resolve problems. Furthermore, corporal punishment can lead to lower self-esteem, increased juvenile delinquency, and increased drug and alcohol use.

12   Parents sometimes feel that their teen's behavior is driven solely by the desire to anger them when it often has nothing to do with them. Even when parents realize they are not responsible for causing their child's behavior, they wonder how their teen could embarrass them if he or she loved them. Effective parenting does not mean getting your teen to express his love for you all the time. It means modeling healthy behavior, creating a safe environment, and allowing your child to find his own path.

13   Anna's behavior at the board meeting when she darted out in anger and embarrassment is similar to Nick's behavior at school when he ran out of Ms. Blackmun's office, also feeling angry and embarrassed. Children model both the healthy and unhealthy behaviors of their parents. Teenagers will learn more by observing their parents' behaviors than by listening to their lectures.

14   One of the ways teens get attention and/or express their individuality is by their mode of dress. They tend to see a parent's harsh judgments about their appearance as an attack on their individuality, and, to assert their independence from that parent, will turn what should have been a minor issue into a major power struggle. Parents who are embarrassed or become angry about their teen's dress (with the possible exception of overly-provocative clothing) are missing a chance to enjoy one of their child's most colorful expressions of individuality. Although there are some exceptions, the way teens dress and how they keep their rooms are probably two of the most unnecessary battles teens and parents engage in.

15   It is common for a teen to act more responsibly and maturely outside the home environment. Parents are often pleasantly surprised to find that their child, who resists doing chores or homework, is a hard worker at an after-school job or voluntarily helps a friend's mother with her yard work. Acquiring a job on his own or offering to do something without being asked can give a teen a sense of ownership that may be missing from school and home, where parents and teachers often tell him what to do and then nag him to do it.

16   It is easy for parents to find themselves drawn into their teen's dramas as if they were their own. The teen will most likely rebel against his parents when they do this, feeling as if they are trying to control his life.

A remedy is to ask, "Whose problem is this?" If the teen owns the problem (for example, he isn't prepared for a test, he has a conflict with a peer, or he's late for work) then it is the teen who should decide when and how to handle it. A parent can offer guidance and support if the teen is responsive and seeking it. However, too often parents attempt to force their ideas and solutions onto their teen and wonder why he won't take their good advice.

Although the advice may be good, the teen is trying to walk his own path and learn from his mistakes. This is a healthy and normal part of adolescence.

17 Although they will fight fiercely for independence, teens are also afraid of it. Like babies learning to walk, they are trying different steps towards adulthood. A skillful parent can see beyond oppositional behavior to the scared but courageous person making the necessary transition into a new phase of life. When teens do open up and tell their parent about a particular problem, often they just want a supportive ear and not to be told what to do. This is different from younger children who typically are asking for a solution.

Chapter Three

18 Letting go of assuming responsibility for your teenager can be trying when he is acting so irresponsibly. However, at a time when your child is learning to become more independent, it is important for him to experience the consequences of his actions, both pro and con. Your teen is likely to take full responsibility only when he realizes that you will not rescue him. Some examples include: not waking him up, even if it means he will miss the bus; not doing his laundry, even if it means he'll have no clean clothes; and not reminding him to do his homework, even if it means it won't get done. Although it is not necessarily counterproductive to wake up your teen, do his laundry, or ask him about his homework, doing so on a consistent basis does not teach independence and may be met with opposition by your adolescent. This is especially true for older teens.

19 When you look in the mirror what do you see? The images that we have of ourselves (both good and bad) influence how we relate to others, including, of course, our teenage children.

20 Physical and emotional space is something that parents and teenagers both need at home-especially during a crisis. Parents have to learn to offer their teens space when they need it, and assert their own need for space when their children invade it.

Chapter Four

21 Too often we get stuck on negative probabilities rather than looking at the exciting possibilities. For example, rather than assuming that a situation will be stressful, try and make yourself see that a positive outcome is just as likely.

22 To see something as already happening can be very helpful in creating it. For example, if you want to be a more compassionate and understanding parent, begin to create a picture of yourself that way. Try to imagine how a compassionate and understanding parent would react in different situations, how they would feel. The more you hold onto these thoughts and images, the more likely you are to produce the desired result.

23   Meditation, an accepted healing technique for thousands of years in Eastern cultures, is now gaining acceptance in the West as a scientifically-proven method for lowering blood pressure, slowing heart rate, and relaxing the mind. At its best, regular meditation can significantly improve the quality of one's life. There are many different types of meditation, all with their own merits. "Mindfulness meditation" is the form Hawk teaches Anna. Through conscious awareness of the thoughts, images, feelings and sensations of the mind, mindfulness meditation helps the regular practitioner gain greater insight and ultimately achieve greater joy and peace of mind.

24   Surprising your teenager with nonjudgmental acceptance at a time when he or she is expecting a scolding can be a powerful way to improve your relationship and their behavior. Keeping sight of the bigger picture-that your teen needs your unconditional love and acceptance, not your advice and judgments-can go a long way toward healing rifts between you.

25   Although running away from tough situations and avoiding recurring issues is counterproductive to maturing and becoming more responsible, an occasional gesture, like what Ms. Blackmun does for Nick by taking him out of Spanish class, can make a teenager feel understood and supported. Situations that have been consistently met with resistance may best be dealt with by changing the situation first, then looking for other ways to help a teen resolve similar conflicts in the future.

26   Developing greater self-awareness can have a direct, positive effect on your relationship with your teenager. It is less threatening and easier for a teen to hear parental judgments when the teen's parents own their own inadequacies and model the ways they themselves are attempting to improve.

Chapter Five

27   Parents who have historically taken more responsibility than necessary for their child's actions often find themselves in a Catch-22 when the child reaches the teen years. If the parent suddenly lets go of his role (e.g., by not driving his daughter to school when she is late), the teen is sure to fail (e.g., not making it to school). However, if the parent continues to bail out his child, she never learns or accepts responsibility for her own behavior. A rule of thumb for parents: if your child can do something for herself, then she should. If you find that you've been doing more than necessary for her, begin to ease off. Have a conversation about how the two of you can work together to help her toward greater independence, develop a plan together, then follow through.

28   Ideally, Anna would have worked out an agreement with Nick and school ahead of time since getting to school on time was a consistent problem. It is reasonable to expect a teen to find his own ride to school if he misses

the bus. If the family lives far from school with no access to public transportation or a taxi, a parent might agree to take the teen as long as he is held accountable in some way. For example, the teen might pay an agreed amount of cab fare to the parent and do an extra chore that night to honor the parent's time. Although offering your teen a ride occasionally can be a nice gesture, a stricter method of accountability may be necessary for the repeat offender.

29 Many conflicts between older teens and their parents are subconsciously motivated by the teens' fear that they are not ready to face the world outside the comforts of the home and by the parents' fear that they are "losing" their little boy or little girl. By openly and honestly communicating your feelings to your child and reassuring her of her ability to make it in the outside world, you can help alleviate some of these fears.

30 Character traits or behaviors of teens that parents despise the most are often triggers for sensitive areas within the parent - either because of her upbringing or her character flaws. This is why friends and other family members might say, "You two are so much alike." Recognizing the similarities can help the parent focus on changing her own shortcomings rather than judging and condemning her child's.

31 Raising children to be responsible, independent, loving adults is a tough job that doesn't come with a manual. While you need not blame yourself for your child's misbehaviors, the more effective you are at managing your own life, the better role model you become and the more you will be able to assist your teen in managing life's ups and downs. Parents who learn to lead healthier, more peaceful lives will pass these benefits on to their children.

32 It is normal adolescent behavior to test limits and question authority. Although parents may feel threatened by this, it is a necessary part of the growth process and a method in which teens develop their own sense of right and wrong. Questioning parental decisions helps an adolescent understand the reasons for the limits they impose and gives a teen the opportunity to participate more fully in those decisions. Respecting your child's role as an instigator of change will help him respect your role as a parent.

33 Complaining that your teen is "ruining" your life identifies you as a victim and your teen as the antagonist and will only add to the conflict between the two of you. Taking responsibility for your life helps you let go of the victim identity and empowers you to make positive change.

34 Effective parenting requires you to separate your needs from those of your teen. As children grow older, parents must gradually let go of control, realizing that their child's destiny is not entirely in their hands.

35 Children need to be reminded that their parents love them. This is especially true in the teen years when conflicts abound between the generations. Since teens are often suspicious of the motivation behind adult behaviors, parents must find creative, subtle ways of expressing their

love. For example, without being asked, you can place a fresh drink next to your teen when she's studying (or watching TV for that matter), or you can send her a surprise email that just says, "You're awesome" (don't sign it). Little gestures like this can be especially powerful if done unexpectedly, such as when your child knows you are angry with her.

Chapter Six

36 Although loving and accepting oneself totally and without judgment is more an ideal than an obtainable goal for most, the degree to which you love and accept yourself is the degree to which you can love and accept others, including your teenage children.

37 There are an infinite number of reasons why humans behave the way they do-personality, prior experiences, knowledge, attitudes and beliefs, the context of a situation, the dynamics of relationships, medical conditions, hormonal activity, diet, self-esteem, self-confidence, and motivation, to name but a few. Blaming your teens for their shortcomings does little to help them grow. Holding them accountable for their behaviors, while loving and supporting them as they seek ways to improve themselves, is a far more effective strategy to promote positive change.

38 Decisions that parents make based on fear are usually ineffective. Fearful parents can "awfulize" a teen's behavior by taking it to the extreme (e.g., "If Jimmy doesn't study, he's going to fail, and if he fails, he's not going to get into a good college, and he'll be a screw-up his entire life...so I have to get on his case about his homework."). Although you shouldn't simply ignore your teen's problems, you could help him toward independence by showing faith that he can solve them himself and by assuring him that he is ultimately going to be okay.

39 Letting your teenager know that you love her in spite of her misbehaviors typically does not lead the teen to think that you condone the behavior-rather, she feels supported in finding a better way to live her life.

40 From past experience, Nick expects his mother to yell at him for his bad grade in Spanish. Parents who focus on the worst part of a report card before praising its positive aspects can have unrealistic expectations for their child. Underachievement in school often occurs when a child rebels against parents who consistently nag about schoolwork. Sharing your genuine interest and concern about your teen's accomplishments and failures without yelling, judging, or condemning her can open up a dialogue between parent and child and improve the teen's attitude and efforts.

41 When parents get into power struggles with their teen, they sometimes get hung up on their own need to win an argument and get their way, losing site of the original goal of teaching the child to be responsible. Punishment meted out by a parent in the heat of the moment probably won't change a

teen's behavior (e.g., grounding for poor grades), but rewards, along with natural and logical consequences, will (e.g., getting a tutor and finding a way to recognize the teen's progress, turning a negative experience into a positive one). Next time you find yourself in a power struggle with your teen, ask yourself, "What's my goal here?" If it is to win the argument and punish your child, then it may be time to rethink your strategy.

42 Identifying with a teenager's problems by sharing similar struggles you experienced as a child can be far more effective in strengthening the relationship than yelling at or scolding her. Too often well-meaning parents try to teach a lesson when their teen is really just looking for someone to listen to her and support her.

Chapter Seven

43 It is natural for parents to want the best for their children. In the early years, this means making most of the important decisions for them. As an adult, you probably have more experience and perhaps greater insight into difficult situations that will arise for your teenagers. Regardless, it is important to allow your teenager to discover her own solutions. By gradually "handing over control" of your teen's life to her, you can do wonders in helping her to become independent and responsible. As she solves more and more of her own problems and realizes that she is able to successfully recover from the poor choices she makes, your adolescent is likely to feel better and better about herself.

44 Teenagers often conspire with each other to deceive their parents; for example, by saying they are sleeping over at a friend's house when they are planning to be elsewhere. It takes a community to raise a teen. Communicating regularly with other parents can help avoid problematic situations. Starting a parent network and holding periodic events with other parents can go a long way in preventing future problems.

45 Teens misbehave because they are testing boundaries in their quest to define who they are. Parents who take personal offense and believe that their teens should not misbehave out of respect for them are using faulty logic. By depersonalizing their teen's misbehavior, parents can handle the situation more rationally.

Chapter Eight

46 Following your heart means acting with compassion, sensitivity, and faith rather than reacting with fear. Ask yourself the question, "What would a loving parent do now?"

47 Parents who feel guilty for ignoring the needs of their child sometimes overcompensate by failing to hold him accountable for his behavior. Do not

replace empathy (putting yourself in your child's shoes) with sympathy (feeling sorry for your child, and thus attempting to overcompensate).

48   Anna's decision not to lecture or punish Nick for smoking weed was a tactful maneuver intended to use Nick's own conscience to prevent future drug use. Although this would not be the best approach in every situation (e.g., if Nick had an increasing drug problem), it holds Nick primarily responsible for his behavior and sends the message that his mother has faith that he will make healthier decisions in the future.

49   Rather than punishing Nick, Anna expresses concern about the loss of trust in their relationship. Asking teens how they can begin to rebuild trust, how they can take responsibility for a wrongdoing, or what they are going to do differently next time is much different and more effective than lecturing them about their irresponsible behaviors or punishing them. The more you are able to include your teen in the discipline and behavior change process, the more likely he is to take ownership and follow through.

50   Anna's consequence for Nick's behavior is logical-it makes sense or "fits the crime." Natural and logical consequences are different than punishment. The former is present and future-based, attempting to avoid similar problems in the future, whereas the latter is past-based, getting revenge for a child's misbehavior. For example, grounding a child for the summer after he takes your car for a joy ride is punishment; withholding rides (making him find his own way to school, soccer practice and the mall) is a logical consequence and "fits the crime." Logical or natural consequences and rewarding positive behavior are more likely to lead to positive behavior change (e.g., showing greater respect for others' property) than punishment, which often just temporarily suppresses negative behavior.

Chapter Nine

51   Misfortune happens to all of us. Approaching misfortunes as a victim is likely to leave one feeling powerless, frustrated, and helpless. Seeking out a higher meaning or purpose in the suffering can lead to a greater sense of control and relief. Remember that crisis is opportunity. Just as young teens experience growing pains as their bodies mature, parents too must experience growing pains in order to achieve a higher awareness and appreciation of self.

52   By keeping an open-mind, you will gain knowledge and wisdom from many sources to help you in raising your teenager—friends, strangers, songs, poems, even your own child. Hopefully this book has been such a resource for you.

Book Ordering Information

To order additional copies of *Finding the Path: A Novel for Parents of Teenagers*, fill out the form below and mail it with your payment to:

Finding the Path
c/o Hawk Mountain Press
P.O. Box 1721
Norristown, PA 19404-1721

Name: _____

Company or Educational Institution: _____

Address: _____

City, State, Zip: _____

E-mail Address: _____

Phone: _____

Other convenient ways to order more copies of *Finding the Path*:
    E-mail: *orders@manageteens.com*
    visit: *www.manageteens.com*
    fax: (206) 666-HAWK (4295)

Payment Information

_____ Number of copies @ $14.95 each   _____
    (Special discounts for orders of 10 or more.
    Call or e-mail for more information)

    6% sales tax for Pennsylvania residents   _____

    Shipping and handling   _____
    ($5 for first book, $2 each additional)

                            TOTAL   _____

_____ Check/Money Order (Payable to: Finding the Path)

_____ Credit Card (circle one)   *MasterCard*   *VISA*   *AMEX*   *Discover*

Name of cardholder as it appears on card: _____

Credit Card Number: _____

Expiration Date: _____

Cardholder Signature: _____

Telephone-based Classes for Parents of Teenagers

Improve your parenting skills, be part of a supportive community of other parents, and receive expert advice...all from the comfort and convenience of your own home. With state-of-the-art phone conferencing technology you can have access to experts with a simple phone call. Telephone-based courses run for four weeks, helping you develop the skills taught in *Finding the Path*.

Love-based Parenting Level I (4 weeks)
> Love vs. fear-based parenting
> Why teens misbehave
> Discipline that works
> Effective communication

Love-based Parenting Level II (4 weeks)*
> School achievement
> Special topics: drugs and alcohol, lying and stealing, delinquency
> Self-esteem and self-image
> Community support

*Open only to graduates of Level I class

To learn more, visit *www.manageteens.com*, send an email to *classes@manageteens.com*, or call (206) 666-HAWK (4295) and leave a message.

_._ _._ _._ _._ _._ _._ _._ _._ _._ _._ _._ _._ _._ _._ _._ _._

FREE Special Topic Teleclass Coupon

By purchasing this book you are entitled to participate for FREE in an upcoming 45-minute **Special Topic Teleclass** offered by Dr. Kaplan (a $99 value). Topics include parent favorites such as effective communication, discipline, drugs and alcohol, and school achievement. Send us the information requested in the form below either by fax, e-mail* or regular mail, and we will contact you with a course schedule.

Name: _____

Address: _____

City, State, Zip: _____

E-mail Address: _____

Phone: _____

Fax: _____

Mail form to Finding the Path, c/o Hawk Mountain Press, P.O. Box 1721, Norristown, PA 19404-1721, fax to (206) 666-HAWK (4295), e-mail to *drjeff@manageteens.com*.

* Be sure to put "Free Teleclass Offer" in the subject line of your e-mail. In the body of the e-mail, type the code **PARENTOFTEEN** to receive this free offer.

Free On-line Newsletter

Get helpful ideas and articles on issues related to parenting teenagers automatically delivered FREE right to your e-mail address. Written and edited by professionals and parents together, *ParenTeen News* is an on-line resource covering a wide variety of issues that parents of teenagers want to know about. Recent issues focused on stress, recreational drug use, teen rebellion, peer pressure, Internet safety, dealing with tragedy, body image, and parent-teen communication.

To receive *ParenTeen News,* visit *www.manageteens.com* and click on the "Sign up for our Free Newsletter" box located in the top right corner.

Speakers' Bureau, Workshops and Retreats

Dr. Kaplan and "Supermom" Abby Lederman are known for their dynamic lectures and programs. They facilitate shorter "brown bag lunch" programs such as "Thirty minutes to a better relationship with your teen," half- and full-day programs such as "Stress management for parents of teenagers" and "Gender issues in parenting teens" and two-day retreats such as "Getting the drama back on track: A retreat for parents of teenagers."

For a complete list of workshops or to have a presentation tailored to your group's individual needs, fill out the form below and send it to:

Speakers' Bureau
Hawk Mountain Press
P.O. Box 1721
Norristown, PA 19404-1721

Name: _____

Company or educational institution: _____

Address: _____

City, State, Zip: _____

E-mail Address: _____

Phone: _____

Fax: _____

Workshop purpose: _____

Possible dates for event: _____

Other convenient ways to get information about workshops and retreats:
E-mail contents of form to: *info@manageteens.com*
Call and leave a voice message or fax: (206) 666-HAWK (4295)